FORBIDDEN WORLDS

By: EDWARD FREEMAN

Published by Edward Freeman

Dedication:

To the readers who dare to venture into the darkest corners of their imaginations, to those who find solace in the grotesque, and to the shadows that whisper secrets only the night understands. This book is a testament to the enduring power of fear, the seductive allure of the unknown, and the resilience of the human spirit, even in the face of unimaginable horror. It is dedicated to you, the intrepid explorers of the forbidden realms within and without. May these pages both terrify and enlighten you, leading you down winding paths where sanity is a fragile thing and the line between nightmare and reality blurs into oblivion. This is a tribute to the darkness that dwells within us all, the darkness that, when confronted, can forge strength, resilience, and an understanding of the very essence of human experience. For within the deepest shadows reside the most profound truths, truths that can shape, alter, and ultimately redefine our perception of ourselves and the world around us. To you, the brave, the curious, the haunted – this is your descent into the abyss.

Preface

The genesis of "Forbidden Worlds" lies not in a single, eureka moment, but in a slow, insidious creep of shadows across the landscape of my imagination. It began with a fascination with the grotesque – not simply as a spectacle of horror, but as a reflection of the hidden, often repulsive aspects of humanity itself. The monstrous creatures within these pages are not merely fantastical creations; they are born from the darkest corners of the human psyche, manifested in forms both terrifying and strangely beautiful. This novel is an exploration of those hidden fears, the anxieties that gnaw at the edges of our consciousness, and the primal forces that shape our world. The unsettling atmosphere, the suspenseful pacing, and the intricate plot are all carefully constructed to draw the reader into Elias Thorne's descent into madness and despair. His journey is not a simple tale of good versus evil; it is a complex exploration of morality, sacrifice, and the ambiguous nature of heroism in a world teetering on the brink of annihilation. I aimed to craft a narrative that is both deeply unsettling and intellectually stimulating, a journey through the darkest depths of the human experience that resonates long after the final page is turned. My hope is that "Forbidden Worlds" will not only entertain but also challenge the reader to confront their own inner demons and grapple with the unsettling truths that lie beneath the surface of reality.

Introduction

Elias Thorne is not your typical hero. He is a man fractured by a past he can barely remember, haunted by whispers from a realm beyond human comprehension. He is a reluctant participant in a cosmic struggle, a pawn in a game played by entities far older and more powerful than himself. "Forbidden Worlds" follows his descent into a nightmarish landscape where the boundaries between reality and the supernatural are shattered. This is not a world of clear-cut morality; it is a twisted reflection of our own, where monstrous creatures are as complex as the humans they prey upon. The narrative explores the insidious corruption that seeps into the very fabric of existence, twisting the familiar into the horrifying and forcing Elias to confront not only external threats but also the terrifying truths hidden within his own soul. Prepare to journey into a realm where shadows dance and whispers turn into screams. Prepare for betrayals that cut deeper than any blade, for sacrifices that leave indelible scars, and for horrors that will linger in your mind long after you've finished reading. This is a story of survival, not just of the physical kind, but of the soul's desperate struggle to remain whole in the face of unimaginable dread. It's a descent into madness and a desperate fight for sanity, all set against a backdrop of grotesque beauty and terrifying wonder. Elias's story is a mirror reflecting the darkest aspects of humanity, a stark reminder of the fragility of our reality and the monstrous potential that lies dormant within us all.

TABLE OF CONTENTS

Chapter 1:
The Cryptic Artifact

The air hung thick with the scent of dust and decay, a miasma clinging to the forgotten corners of the Blackwood Museum. Elias Thorne, his trench coat collar pulled high against the chill despite the summer heat outside, felt a tremor of unease, a familiar prickling at the edges of his awareness. He wasn't here for the dusty relics of bygone eras; he was chasing a ghost, a phantom of a memory that flickered at the edge of his consciousness, a memory both vivid and elusive. His breath hitched as he navigated the labyrinthine corridors, the silence broken only by the rhythmic drip, drip, drip of a leaky pipe echoing in the oppressive quiet. He felt watched, the hairs on the back of his neck standing on end.

He'd stumbled upon a reference to the museum in a decaying journal, a cryptic note mentioning a "key," a "gateway," and a symbol he'd only ever seen in his nightmares – a twisted, obsidian serpent coiled around a skull.

The symbol had haunted his dreams since childhood, a recurring motif in the fragmented memories that plagued him, memories that felt both his own and utterly alien.

The museum itself seemed to lean in on him, its decaying walls whispering secrets of forgotten horrors. Peeling paint flaked from the ceilings, revealing glimpses of the brickwork beneath, a brickwork stained with what looked disturbingly like dried blood. The displays were haphazard, cobweb-draped, the artifacts appearing more like forgotten victims than relics of the past.

He found it in a shadowed alcove, tucked away behind a crumbling display case overflowing with chipped porcelain dolls. It was small, no larger than his palm, an object of unsettling beauty. Made of a dark,
polished stone that seemed to absorb the scant light in the alcove, it pulsed with a faint, internal luminescence, a sickly green glow that seemed to writhe beneath its surface. Runes, unlike any language he knew, were etched into its surface, their glyphs unsettlingly familiar, a chilling echo of the serpent symbol from his dreams. He reached out, a tremor in

his hand, feeling the cold smoothness of the stone against his fingertips.

As his fingers brushed the surface, a low hum resonated through the artifact, a vibration that seemed to burrow into his very bones. The air around him crackled with unseen energy, the temperature plummeting despite the already chilly atmosphere. The hum intensified, growing into a deafening roar that seemed to tear the fabric of reality itself. His vision blurred, the world around him twisting and warping, the walls of the museum melting away into a chaotic swirl of color and shadow.

He stumbled, the artifact slipping from his grasp, landing with a dull thud on the floor. The ground beneath his feet dissolved, replaced by a bottomless chasm of swirling darkness. He felt a sickening lurch in his stomach, a sensation of falling through an eternity of night.

When his senses began to return, he found himself standing in a place that defied description, a landscape born of nightmare. Towering spires of jagged obsidian pierced a sky the color of bruised flesh, casting long, skeletal shadows across a blighted land. The air throbbed with an oppressive silence, broken only by the occasional shriek of unseen creatures. The very ground beneath his feet seemed to writhe, the earth itself alive with a malevolent energy.

He was no longer in the museum; the familiar stench of dust and decay had been replaced by a cloying odor, a sickening sweetness mixed with the metallic tang of blood. The air was heavy with the palpable presence of something ancient and profoundly evil.

Twisted, grotesque trees clawed at the sky, their branches gnarled and skeletal, their leaves the color of dried blood. In the distance, monstrous shapes moved, their forms obscured by the perpetual twilight, but their presence was undeniable. He caught glimpses of chittering, insectile things, their bodies a horrifying fusion of chitin and flesh, and towering figures that seemed sculpted from shadow itself. They were impossibly tall and thin, their limbs like gnarled branches reaching out from bodies that appeared to be made of nothing more than darkness.

Terror gripped him, cold and paralyzing. This was not a dream; this was something far more real, far more terrifying. He had stumbled upon something beyond human comprehension, something ancient and utterly malevolent. The artifact, the key, had opened a gate to a realm that existed beyond the confines of his reality, a realm of unimaginable horror.

The artifact, still lying on the ground, pulsed with a renewed intensity, the green glow now brighter, more menacing. He had to get away, yet an irresistible curiosity held him rooted to the spot. The weight of his fragmented past began to press upon him, as if the memories, so long suppressed, now poured forth in a torrent of chaotic images. He saw fleeting glimpses of a ceremony, of a sacrifice, of a symbol identical to the one etched onto the artifact. He saw faces, twisted and monstrous,

yet undeniably familiar. He felt a connection to this place, to this forbidden realm, a connection that chilled him to the core.

Then, from the shadows, a figure emerged. It was tall and slender, cloaked in darkness, its face obscured by a deep hood. The figure moved with an unnerving grace, its movements fluid and silent, like the passage of smoke. It did not seem to walk, but rather to glide across the blighted landscape, its feet never seeming to touch the ground.

As it approached, Elias could sense an aura of power radiating from it, a palpable presence that spoke of an age beyond human reckoning. The creature stopped before him, its presence filling him with a sense of both dread and an inexplicable fascination. The hood shifted slightly, revealing a glimpse of a face that defied description – a face sculpted from shadow and bone, with eyes that glowed with an infernal light.

It spoke, its voice a resonant whisper that seemed to echo in the very depths of Elias's soul. The words were not of this world, yet somehow, he understood. It spoke of ancient conflicts, of a war between worlds, of a gateway that should never have been opened. It spoke of power, of betrayal, and of the inevitable darkness that awaited him.

It offered both a warning and a cryptic clue, a fragment of knowledge that further fueled his terrifying journey. The entity spoke of a forgotten civilization, a race that had once held dominion over this nightmarish realm, and of the entities that sought to usurp their power. It hinted at Elias's own role in this ancient conflict, a role he had long since forgotten, a role that he was now inexorably bound to play.

The cryptic words lingered in the air, a chilling promise of horrors yet to come. Elias, the man haunted by a fragmented past, now found himself inextricably entwined with a future even more terrifying. He had touched the artifact, and in doing so, he had touched the very heart of darkness. The gateway was open, and his descent into the abyss had begun. The weight of the unknown pressed down on him, a suffocating burden of impending doom, yet somewhere deep within, a flicker of defiance ignited. He was more than a pawn in a cosmic game, he was Elias Thorne, and he would fight. He had to. The fate of two worlds hung in the balance.

The cold, metallic surface of the artifact pulsed faintly beneath his fingertips, a tremor that resonated not just in the object itself, but deep within Elias's bones. It felt...alive. A low hum, almost imperceptible at first, grew in intensity, vibrating through his hand and up his arm, a chilling melody that seemed to burrow into his very soul. The air around him crackled with an unnatural energy, the scent of ozone mixing with the stale museum air, creating a nauseating cocktail that burned his nostrils.

The darkness that had previously been a lurking presence in the corners of the room intensified, coalescing into a swirling vortex of shadows before him. It was not simply darkness; it was an absence, a void that seemed to pull at his very being, threatening to tear him apart

at the molecular level. He felt a primal fear, a terror so deep and visceral it transcended reason, a sense of utter insignificance in the face of an unimaginable power. He tried to pull his hand away, but an unseen force held it captive, drawing him closer to the heart of the maelstrom.

The hum intensified, becoming a deafening roar that threatened to shatter his eardrums. Colors, impossible, grotesque colors, began to bleed into the periphery of his vision. Crimson, the color of dried blood, blended with a sickly green, the hue of phosphorescent decay, and a shimmering, opalescent white that pulsed with an unnatural light. The vortex twisted and writhed, its surface rippling like disturbed water, revealing glimpses of something...other.

Silhouettes flickered within the swirling darkness – monstrous shapes, barely discernible at first, yet growing ever clearer, more defined as the gateway expanded. Long, spindly limbs, tipped with claws that seemed sharper than any earthly blade, reached out from the abyss, grasping at the air as if trying to pull themselves into this world. Eyes, vast and malevolent, like burning coals in the depths of hell, fixated on Elias, burning with an unholy hunger. He glimpsed glimpses of flesh – or something that resembled flesh – twisted and contorted in impossible angles, suggesting forms both organic and inorganic, a nightmarish fusion of nature's worst nightmares.

One creature, more distinct than the others, began to emerge from the swirling chaos. It was tall and gaunt, its skeletal frame draped in tattered, decaying robes that seemed to shift and reform in the turbulent air. Its head was elongated, a skull-like structure with eyes that glowed with an eerie luminescence. Its hands ended not in fingers but in wickedly curved talons that dripped with a viscous, black ichor. The creature let out a shriek that was not sound but a vibration of pure, unadulterated evil, a resonance that penetrated his very being, shaking him to his core.

The other monstrous forms seemed to obey this leader, their movements synchronized in a grotesque ballet of dread. They were diverse, a menagerie of horrors. Some were serpentine, slithering creatures with scales of obsidian and eyes like chips of ice. Others were hulking behemoths, their bodies a grotesque amalgamation of flesh and bone, moving with a terrifying grace that defied their immense size. Still others possessed no discernible form, appearing as amorphous blobs of pulsating darkness, their presence a palpable threat of cosmic annihilation.

As the gateway widened, the air grew heavier, the pressure increasing, pushing against Elias with an almost unbearable weight. The stench intensified, a vile mixture of decay, sulfur, and something else, something ancient and primordial, that invoked the deepest recesses of his subconscious – a scent of dread he somehow recognized from the forgotten edges of his own mind. He felt himself being pulled towards the gateway, the vortex's irresistible pull overcoming his will, his fear, and his desperate fight for survival.

He struggled, clawing at the air, at the stone floor, at anything that would provide a purchase against the overwhelming force. But his efforts were futile. The pull was relentless, a tide of darkness that swept him off his feet, dragging him towards the abyss, a sacrifice to the nightmare that unfurled before him.

The world twisted and turned, colors bled and blurred, and then... darkness. A darkness not merely the absence of light, but

an oppressive, suffocating entity that pressed
in from all sides.

He felt a searing pain, as if his very
being were being torn asunder. His senses
were overwhelmed by a cacophony of screams,
whispers, and grinding sounds, a chorus of
unimaginable horrors that seemed to echo

from the edges of existence. The air
vibrated with a malevolent energy, a symphony
of chaos and destruction.
And then, just as suddenly as it had
begun, the pain subsided. He opened his eyes,
his vision slowly clearing. He was no longer in
the dusty confines of the Blackwood Museum.

He found himself standing on a
precipice of a landscape that defied description.
The ground beneath his feet was cracked and
barren, a desolate expanse of twisted rock
formations, the colors a sickly yellow and a
bruised purple. The sky was a swirling vortex
of crimson and black, a perpetual twilight that
cast long, distorted shadows across the land.
In the distance, he saw structures that seemed
to defy the laws of physics – towers of obsidian

that scraped the tormented sky, their surfaces covered in strange, pulsating symbols.

The creatures he had glimpsed in the gateway were everywhere, moving with unnatural grace, their forms blending seamlessly with the harsh landscape. He saw the skeletal figure, its eyes burning into him, its presence commanding a dreadful respect. It was surveying its domain, an absolute ruler over this desolate kingdom.

The air was thick with a palpable sense of dread, a chilling silence broken only by the occasional shriek of a monstrous creature or the rhythmic drip of some viscous, unknown substance. This was a world of perpetual twilight, where the sun never shone and the moon never set, a land of eternal night. This was the forbidden world, a realm beyond human comprehension, a nightmare given tangible form.

A cold realization washed over Elias. He hadn't merely opened a gateway; he had torn a gaping wound in the fabric of reality, releasing a horde of creatures that threatened to spill into his world. His initial fear gave way to a chilling sense of responsibility. He had done this. The weight of the world, or perhaps multiple worlds, now rested on his shoulders.

He looked back towards the gateway, half-expecting to see a way back, but there was only the endless, desolate landscape. The portal had closed behind him, leaving him stranded in this nightmarish realm. The weight of his actions pressed down upon him, a suffocating burden of impending doom. But unlike the terror of the abyss, this new burden also came with a surge of fierce determination. He would find a way to seal the gateway, even if it meant facing unimaginable horrors. He had to. The fate of two worlds depended on it. His descent into hell had

just begun. And he would not go down without a fight. He had to find out what kind of hell this place was, and how to escape. The journey, he suspected, would be longer and more harrowing than he could possibly imagine.

The monstrous creatures, sensing his presence, began to approach, their movements slow and deliberate, their eyes fixed on him with a hunger that was both primal and terrifying. Elias knew that his first battle in this forbidden realm had begun. The survival of his world – and possibly his own soul – depended upon his victory. He drew a deep breath, the cold, stale air burning his lungs, and met their gaze with a steely resolve. He was Elias Thorne, and he would not surrender. Not now. Not ever. The fight for survival was far from over. This was only the beginning of the end.

The creatures surged, a tide of chittering limbs and snapping jaws, their forms a grotesque mockery of earthly life. One, larger than the others, its skin a patchwork of decaying flesh and glistening chitin, lunged, its mandibles clicking like a clockwork death. Elias reacted instinctively, the training he'd undergone as a former special forces operative kicking in. He rolled, dodging the snapping jaws by a hair's breadth, the creature's claws raking across the stone floor inches from his face. The air vibrated with the sounds of the struggle – the rasping breaths of the

beasts, the scrape of their claws, the dull thud of his body hitting the cold stone.

He scrambled to his feet, his heart hammering against his ribs, adrenaline flooding his system. The artifact, still clutched in his hand, throbbed with a frantic energy, its metallic surface burning against his skin. It felt like a living thing, reacting to the danger, feeding off the fear and desperation that coursed through his veins. He wasn't just fighting for survival; the artifact itself seemed to be fighting alongside him.

Suddenly, a voice cut through the cacophony of the battle, a voice that resonated not in his ears but deep within his mind. It was a voice ancient, weary, and laced with an unnerving wisdom. It spoke in a language he didn't understand, yet somehow, he comprehended its meaning, a direct translation occurring within his consciousness.

"Foolish mortal," the voice echoed. "You have awakened forces beyond your comprehension. The gateway is open, and the hunger is insatiable."

Elias stumbled back, the creatures momentarily distracted by the ethereal intrusion. He looked around, desperately searching for the source of the voice, but found nothing. The museum hall remained unchanged, the only light emanating from the artifact itself, casting long, dancing shadows that writhed like sentient things.

"Who...who are you?" Elias managed, his voice a hoarse whisper.

"I am a remnant," the voice replied, "a whisper from the age before time. I have watched the rise and fall of civilizations, the endless cycle of creation and destruction. And now, you, Elias Thorne, are caught in the current of this ancient war."

The creatures renewed their assault, their movements coordinated now, their attacks more precise. Elias fought back with grim determination, his movements fueled by a primal instinct to survive. He used the artifact as a weapon, its sharp edges tearing through the flesh of his attackers, the metal seeming to glow with an inner light as it connected with its targets. Each blow was accompanied by a low, resonant hum that seemed to amplify the artifact's power.

The being continued to communicate with him telepathically, offering cryptic clues and warnings. It spoke of the "Old Ones," powerful entities who had ruled this realm for eons, their existence predating humanity. It spoke of a conflict that spanned millennia, a struggle for dominance between these ancient beings and the monstrous creatures that now threatened to spill into Elias's world.

"They seek to break the seals," the voice warned, "to unleash a darkness that will consume all. You...you hold the key, Elias Thorne. But the price of wielding such power is steep. You must choose your path wisely."

The battle raged on, Elias finding a strange harmony in the chaos. The artifact pulsed in his hand, its energy surging with every swing, every parry. He felt its power flow through him, strengthening him, sharpening his senses. But with each passing moment, he felt a growing unease, a sense of dread that went beyond the immediate danger of the monstrous creatures.

He was not just fighting for survival; he was becoming a part of something far larger, far older, than he could ever have imagined. The weight of the ages pressed down on him, the burden of a conflict that
threatened to consume not only his world but the very fabric of existence.

As the last of the creatures fell, their bodies dissolving into shimmering dust, Elias collapsed to his knees, exhausted but alive. The artifact pulsed softly in his hand, its glow dimming slightly. The voice was still there, a quiet hum in the back of his mind, a constant reminder of the ancient war he was now a part of.

The voice revealed further details, revealing the true nature of the artifact. It was not just a gateway; it was a key, a fragment of a powerful weapon created by the Old Ones themselves. A weapon that could either seal the gateway permanently, or unleash even greater horrors upon the world.
"The choice is yours, Elias," the voice whispered, its tone laced with a chilling neutrality. "Use this power wisely, for the fate of worlds hangs in the balance."

The weight of that statement, the gravity of his newfound responsibility, pressed down on Elias. He was no longer just a man haunted by his past. He was a warrior, a key player in a cosmic battle

that stretched back eons. He was a
reluctant hero, thrust into a role for which he
was utterly unprepared.

He looked at the artifact, at its cold,
metallic surface, and he felt not only fear, but
also a strange kind of determination. He would
not back down. He would not let the darkness
consume his world. He would fight for survival,
for humanity, even if it meant facing the
unimaginable horrors that lurked just beyond
the veil. He would use the power of the artifact,
even though he knew the cost might be greater
than anything he could ever have imagined.
His survival, and the fate of the world,
depended on it. The weight of the decision, the
potential for both salvation and utter
devastation, pressed down on him, heavier
than the stone floor beneath his knees. The
cold, metallic artifact pulsed softly, a faint
heartbeat in the silent museum hall, a promise,
a threat, and a terrible, breathtaking
responsibility. His journey had begun.
The biting chill of the museum floor
seeped into Elias's bones, a stark contrast to
the sudden, searing heat that flared behind his
eyes. He gasped, a strangled sound lost in the
echoing silence of the ravaged hall. The image
slammed into his mind: a swirling vortex of

crimson and black, a landscape twisted into impossible angles, the air thick with the stench of decay and something else...something ancient and malevolent. He saw figures, monstrous and vaguely humanoid, their

eyes burning with a cold, unnatural light. He heard screams, not of pain, but of something far more primal, a terror that burrowed into the very marrow of his being.

Then, just as swiftly as it began, the vision vanished, leaving him trembling, his breath ragged. His heart hammered against his ribs, a frantic drumbeat in the oppressive stillness. He wasn't sure how long he lay there, the cold stone a stark reminder of his present reality. The artifact, still clutched in his hand, felt strangely warm against his skin, a counterpoint to the icy grip of fear that constricted his chest.

The memory, or whatever it was, felt both alien and intimately familiar. It wasn't simply a nightmare; it was a visceral experience, a glimpse into something horrifically real. The creatures from his vision mirrored the horrors he'd just faced in the museum – the same grotesque anatomy, the same chilling aura of malevolence. A connection solidified within him, a chilling certainty that his past held the key to this terrifying present. He wasn't just an unwitting participant in this struggle; he was somehow intrinsically linked to it.

The flashbacks continued throughout the following days, fragmented and disorienting. One moment, he was a child, hiding in the shadows of

a decaying manor house, the chilling laughter of unseen entities echoing through the vast, empty rooms. He saw a woman, her face obscured by darkness, yet her eyes held an unbearable sorrow, a desperate plea for help that resonated across decades. Another image showed him, older, but still young, undergoing rigorous training, his instructors figures of stern authority and relentless intensity. The training wasn't ordinary; it was brutal, visceral, designed to break him and mold him into something...different. He felt the sting of the whip, the searing pain of the training exercises, but through it all, an undercurrent of something else – a power, a potential that frightened him almost as much as the brutality itself.

The memories felt both real and impossibly surreal, interwoven with fragments of nightmares and half-remembered dreams. He wasn't sure what was fact and what was the product of a fractured mind, fueled by the trauma he'd experienced in the museum. The line between reality and hallucination blurred, becoming almost indistinguishable. His sleep became a torment, filled with nightmarish visions of the forbidden world and the monstrous creatures that inhabited it. He woke drenched in sweat, his heart pounding, the chilling remnants of the visions clinging to him like a shroud.

He sought solace in solitude, retreating to his sparsely furnished apartment, a place he had intentionally kept devoid of personal touches, a fortress against the encroaching darkness within and without. He tried to piece together the fragments of his memories, searching for a common thread, a clue that would unlock the enigma of his past and his seemingly preordained connection to this nightmarish reality. He found nothing concrete, only a growing sense of dread and a disturbing certainty that he was not who he thought he was.

The artifact sat on his desk, a cold, metallic presence. It felt inert now, no longer pulsing with that unsettling energy he had experienced in the museum. Yet, despite its apparent dormancy, he felt a strange pull towards it, a sense of anticipation that bordered on dread. It was a physical manifestation of his uncertain past, a key to a door he wasn't entirely sure he wanted to open.

His research into the artifact yielded little. He'd scoured libraries, archives, and obscure online forums, looking for any mention of the symbol etched onto its surface – a complex glyph that seemed both ancient and alien. His search only served to deepen the mystery. The symbol appeared to have no known origin, no cultural or historical context. It was as if it had been deliberately erased from all records, a testament to its inherent power and the secrets it guarded.

His investigation took him down a rabbit hole of conspiracy theories and forgotten lore, encountering cryptic hints and shadowy figures who seemed to know more than they let on. He encountered whispers of a secret society, an organization that had guarded the gateway to the forbidden world for centuries, protecting humanity from its horrors. But the motives of this society remained unclear, their actions shrouded in secrecy and suspicion. Were they protectors or manipulators, guardians of the world or guardians of a darker power?

The weight of his past, of his burgeoning connection to this otherworldly conflict, began to crush him. The nightmares intensified, the fragmented memories coalescing into terrifyingly coherent narratives, painting a grim portrait of his upbringing and the hidden world he seemed to have been born into. He saw himself as a child, not simply hiding in a decaying house but undergoing secret rituals, being subjected to mysterious ceremonies that instilled within him an uncanny connection to the forbidden world and its horrific denizens.

He was no ordinary man; he was a vessel, a conduit, unknowingly chosen to play a pivotal role in this conflict. He was a key player in a game that stretched back centuries, a game he hadn't even realized he was playing until he stumbled upon the artifact. The realization was both terrifying and strangely liberating. He was no longer a passive observer, a victim of circumstances. He was a participant, albeit an unwilling one. He had a role to play, a destiny to confront, however terrifying it might be.

The artifact, lying cold on his desk, was not just a gateway; it was a reflection of himself, of the hidden depths within him, the suppressed power, the latent potential he didn't know he possessed. It was a tool, a weapon, and a burden. He understood that he had to accept it, embrace it, however horrifying the truth about his past and its implications for his future might be. His journey had only just begun, and the darkness was coming for him, whether he was ready or not. He was no longer merely haunted by his past; he was now its unwilling embodiment, a warrior facing an impossible war against the encroaching forces of a forgotten realm. The shadow of his past was no longer just a haunting; it was his fate. His duty. And the fate of humanity itself.

The weight of the artifact pressed down on Elias, not physically, but with a crushing sense of responsibility. It pulsed faintly in his hand, a rhythmic thrumming that seemed to

echo the frantic beat of his own heart. He'd
seen the glimpse, the horrifying vision of the
forbidden realm, and the memory clung to him
like a shroud. It wasn't just a glimpse; it was a
warning. A chilling premonition of the horrors
he was about to unleash. Yet, the allure was
too strong, the call too insistent. He couldn't
simply ignore it, couldn't bury the artifact and
pretend it wasn't real. The knowledge it held,
the power it promised, was a siren's song,
drawing him into its treacherous depths.

He spent the next few days immersed in
research, poring over ancient texts and
forgotten languages, seeking any clue that
might explain the artifact's origin and purpose.
The library became his sanctuary, a refuge
from the growing unease that gnawed at his
soul. He discovered fragmented accounts of a
civilization that predated recorded history, a
people who had wielded unimaginable power,
mastering forces beyond human
comprehension. Their downfall, the texts
suggested, was a consequence of their hubris,
their reckless pursuit of knowledge beyond
their grasp. The artifact, he realized, was a
remnant of this lost civilization, a key to
unlocking their forbidden secrets.

The research was grueling, a descent
into a labyrinthine world of cryptic symbols
and esoteric rituals. He deciphered passages
that described terrifying entities, beings of pure
shadow and nightmare, whose very existence
defied logic and reason. They were entities that
fed on fear, on despair, their power fueled by
the suffering of others. The texts spoke of a
ritual, a gateway, a means of summoning these
beings into the mortal realm – a gateway that
the artifact seemed to control.

Elias felt a creeping dread, a sense of
impending doom that clung to him like a
second skin. He understood the risk now, the
terrible price of knowledge he was about to pay.
The artifact wasn't just a key; it was a contract,
a pact with forces beyond his comprehension.
He was playing a game with entities far older
and more powerful than himself, entities that
wouldn't hesitate to crush him like an insect if
he failed to meet their demands.

The chilling descriptions of the ritual
haunted his dreams. He saw himself standing
before a gaping chasm, a vortex of swirling
darkness that pulsed with a sickening, organic
rhythm. He saw the monstrous forms
coalescing from the void, their eyes burning

with an unholy light, their mouths dripping with viscous, black ichor. He felt their gaze upon him, cold and calculating, judging his worthiness to wield their power.

He tried to stop, to put the artifact aside, to forget the terrifying knowledge he had unearthed. But the lure was too strong. The weight of responsibility pressed down on him – a responsibility not only to himself, but to humanity as a whole. If this forbidden realm was as dangerous as the ancient texts suggested, then he was the only one who could stop it. He was the only one who could seal the gateway, prevent the apocalyptic incursion.

The next stage of his research took him to the Vatican Secret Archives, a place shrouded in mystery and guarded by centuries of secrecy. He presented himself as a historian, a scholar seeking forgotten knowledge, and after weeks of negotiations and bureaucratic hurdles, he was granted access. The archives were a labyrinth of dimly lit corridors and towering shelves crammed with dusty tomes, ancient manuscripts, and forgotten relics. The air was thick with the scent of old paper and the palpable weight of history.

There, amidst the forgotten chronicles
and suppressed knowledge, he found the
missing pieces of the puzzle. He uncovered a
hidden lineage, a secret society that had
guarded the knowledge of the forbidden realm
for centuries, passing it down through
generations. They were the keepers of the gate,
the protectors of humanity against the
encroaching darkness. And they had failed.

He discovered that the artifact wasn't
unique; there were others, scattered across the
globe, each a key to unlocking a different aspect
of the gateway. The ancient civilization hadn't
simply vanished; they were banished,
imprisoned in the forbidden realm, their power
harnessed and controlled by the monstrous
entities they had summoned. The society had
attempted to seal the gateway, but their efforts
had been in vain. The entities were growing
stronger, their influence spreading, their reach
extending into the mortal realm. The only way
to seal the gateway completely was to perform
the ritual, to use the artifact to banish the
entities back into their prison, but the ritual
was perilous, a gamble with his life and
potentially the lives of everyone else.

Elias felt a profound sense of isolation, a heavy weight of loneliness. He was alone, utterly alone, in his quest to prevent the apocalypse. The secret society was long gone, their knowledge lost or scattered. He couldn't turn to anyone for help; to reveal the truth would only lead to fear, panic, and potentially global chaos. He carried the burden of his knowledge, the crushing weight of responsibility, in complete solitude.

The physical toll was beginning to show. Sleep became a luxury he couldn't afford. The visions plagued him, not only in his dreams, but in his waking hours. He started seeing fragments of the forbidden realm in everyday objects, in the shadows of buildings, in the reflections of mirrors. The line between reality and nightmare was blurring, threatening to consume him entirely.

Yet, amidst the despair and dread, a flicker of defiance ignited within him. He wouldn't surrender. He wouldn't let the darkness consume him or the world. He would fight, even if the odds were insurmountable. He would face the monstrous entities, conquer his own fears, and seal the gateway, whatever the cost. The weight of responsibility, once crushing, now fueled his determination. The price of knowledge was high, but he was willing to pay it. He would not be broken. He would not fail. He had glimpsed the abyss, and now he would stare into its heart, armed with nothing but his own will and the cursed artifact in his trembling hand. The journey to confront this terrifying power was just beginning; it was a race against time, a desperate battle against the encroaching darkness that threatened to swallow the world whole. He was not just fighting for his life, but for the future of humanity itself, a future shrouded in the shadows of an impending apocalypse.

Chapter 2:
Descent into Darkness

The air hung thick and cloying, a miasma of decay and something far older, far more sinister. The ground beneath Elias's boots crunched under a layer of what looked like pulverized bone, mixed with a glistening, black substance that pulsed faintly with an inner light. This was no ordinary landscape; this was a realm sculpted from nightmares, a place where the very fabric of reality seemed to fray at the edges. He'd stumbled through the gateway, a swirling vortex of shadow and light, and now found himself in a landscape that defied description. Towering spires of twisted bone, etched with obscene glyphs, clawed at the perpetually twilight sky. The air itself throbbed with a discordant hum, a symphony of unseen horrors.

His first encounter was with something that slithered from beneath a jagged, obsidian rock. It was a creature of impossible angles and shifting forms, a grotesque parody of a serpent. Its scales, if they could be called that, were shards of black glass, reflecting the dim light in unsettling ways. Each scale seemed to writhe independently, giving the impression that the creature was a living tapestry woven from nightmares. From its gaping maw dripped a viscous, phosphorescent fluid, leaving a trail that glowed faintly in the oppressive darkness. The creature hissed, a sound that resonated deep within Elias's bones, and lunged.

He reacted instinctively, the training he'd received as a soldier kicking in. He rolled away, avoiding the creature's snapping jaws, and drew the ancient dagger he'd found nestled within the artifact. The blade, cold and impossibly sharp, felt alive in his hand. He plunged it into the creature's flank, a sickening crunch accompanying the penetration of its glassy scales. The creature recoiled, emitting a high-pitched shriek that seemed to tear at the very fabric of the air. It writhed for a moment, its body convulsing before collapsing into a pile of shattered glass and that same pulsing black substance.

The experience, though harrowing, was a baptism of fire. It confirmed the perilous nature of this realm, a place where even the smallest creatures possessed a horrifying lethality. He pressed onward, navigating the labyrinthine landscape with a growing sense of dread. The twisted trees, their branches like skeletal fingers reaching for him, seemed to watch him with malevolent curiosity. The ground was treacherous, dotted with treacherous pits and unseen chasms. He had to be vigilant, alert to the slightest shift in the oppressive silence, the slightest whisper of movement in the shadows.

As he journeyed deeper into this abyssal world, the horrors only intensified. He encountered creatures that defied his understanding of biology, entities that seemed to be formed from the very essence of darkness. One was a hulking mass of writhing tentacles, its surface covered in parasitic growths that pulsed rhythmically. Another was a creature composed entirely of shadow, its form shifting and unstable, its presence marked by a chilling coldness that seeped into Elias's very soul. Each encounter tested his resolve, pushing him to the limits of his endurance. Yet, he pressed on, driven by a mixture of fear and a desperate need to understand the nature of this forbidden world, and his own connection to it.

The landscape itself seemed to conspire against him. The ground shifted beneath his feet, the air grew thick with a suffocating fog, and the darkness itself seemed to press in on him, suffocating him both physically and mentally. He felt a creeping despair, a sense of

utter isolation that gnawed at his sanity. The
weight of his past, the fragmented memories
that haunted him, seemed to amplify the
terrors of this realm, blurring the line between
his internal struggles and the external horrors.
He battled not only monstrous creatures but
also the specters of his own mind.

However, amidst the grotesque and
terrifying, he found glimmers of something else
– something unexpected. He discovered subtle
signs of civilization, ruins that spoke of a
forgotten people who had once inhabited this
nightmarish world. The architecture was both
breathtaking and horrifying, a chaotic blend of
organic and geometric forms that reflected the
bizarre ecology of the realm. In these ruins, he
found clues, fragments of history that
illuminated the nature of the ancient conflict
hinted at by the cryptic being he'd met at the
gateway.

In one particularly striking ruin, he
discovered a hidden chamber adorned with
intricate murals. The murals depicted a
civilization that lived in harmony with the
monstrous creatures, a civilization that had
somehow achieved a delicate balance with the
dark forces of this realm. But the murals also

hinted at a cataclysmic event, a war that shattered this harmony, leaving behind only ruin and despair. It was a story of betrayal, of sacrifice, and of a terrifying power that threatened to consume not only this forbidden world, but the mortal realm as well.

As he delved deeper into the mysteries of this forgotten civilization, he began to uncover a centuries-old conspiracy involving powerful entities who sought to control the gateway between worlds. These entities, ancient and malevolent, had manipulated events for centuries, using human ambition and fear as weapons in their quest for dominion. Their goal was to tear down the barrier between the realms, unleashing the horrors of this forbidden world upon humanity. Elias's discovery of the artifact, his unwitting opening of the gateway, had placed him at the center of this ancient conflict, making him a pawn in a game with unimaginable stakes.

The realization dawned on him with a chilling clarity. He wasn't just exploring a dangerous world; he was caught in a war, a war that had raged for centuries, a war that he had inadvertently awakened. The burden of this knowledge, the weight of this responsibility, settled heavily on his shoulders. He was no longer merely a man haunted by his past; he was a reluctant warrior, standing on the precipice of a battle he didn't choose, but one he had to fight. His journey into the forbidden realm had transformed him, stripping away his illusions and forcing him to confront not only the horrors of the outside world, but the darkness that resided within himself. The abyss had stared back, and it had shown him a reflection he couldn't ignore.

His path wasn't just a physical descent into the heart of darkness; it was also a descent into his own psyche, a confrontation with the buried traumas and suppressed memories that had haunted him since his childhood. The monstrous creatures he encountered became a reflection of his inner demons, his fears made manifest in the flesh. The oppressive darkness of this realm mirrored the shadows that had always lingered within him, and the desperate struggle for survival echoed the battles he had waged against himself. His experiences in the forbidden realm were stripping away layers of his identity, revealing a strength and resilience he never knew he possessed, but also a profound loneliness and isolation.

He knew that his journey was far from over. The path ahead was fraught with peril, full of betrayals, sacrifice, and unimaginable horrors. He had already faced a near-fatal encounter with the grotesque serpent-like creature, survived perilous terrain, and deciphered fragments of a civilization's dark history. Yet, even with the horrors he'd endured, he felt a strange resolve hardening within him. The weight of responsibility – the fate of two worlds hanging in the balance – had forged a new purpose within him, a grim determination to fight a war he never asked for. The descent into darkness was far from finished. The abyss awaited, beckoning him deeper into its heart. And Elias, despite his fear and doubt, found himself answering its call.

The landscape was a grotesque parody of nature. Twisted, skeletal trees, their branches gnarled like the limbs of the damned, clawed at the perpetually twilight sky. Their leaves, if they could be called that, were ragged, black things that rustled with a sound like dry bones grinding together. The ground, a shifting carpet of pulverized bone and that unsettling, pulsating black substance, undulated subtly, as if breathing. It wasn't just the ground; the very air seemed alive, a sentient entity that pressed against Elias, whispering secrets of decay and unimaginable suffering.

He saw then, with a horrifying clarity, that the monstrous creatures weren't simply inhabitants of this world; they were integral to its very being. The black substance, he now realized, wasn't just some inert material. It pulsed with a faint, internal light, a bioluminescence that seemed to feed the grotesque flora and fauna of this hellish realm. He watched as a cluster of what appeared to be fungal growths, taller than a man and as thick as a redwood, pulsed with the same black light, their caps releasing a cloud of spores that drifted towards a nearby creature – a hulking monstrosity resembling a cross between a spider and a scorpion, its chitinous shell shimmering with the same eerie glow. The creature absorbed the spores, its form seeming to swell and strengthen as it did so.

This was a twisted symbiosis, a horrifying ecology where predator and prey, parasite and host, were inextricably linked. The very act of predation seemed to enrich the land, fueling the grotesque growth of the landscape itself. The creatures, in their horrifying existence, were not merely surviving; they were actively shaping their environment, creating this nightmarish Eden of decay. He saw smaller, more insect-like creatures scavenging amongst the pulverized bones, their bodies shimmering with the same bioluminescent black light, their movements frantic and seemingly driven by an unseen hunger. They were part of the cycle, contributing to the ceaseless decay and renewal that defined this abhorrent world.

He noticed a pattern emerging. The larger, more powerful creatures, such as the spider-scorpion, occupied the areas where the black substance pulsed most strongly. The smaller, weaker creatures concentrated in areas where the bone-dust was thickest, seemingly sustaining themselves from the remnants of those who had come before. It was a brutal cycle, a constant struggle for survival in a world where death and decay were the driving forces. The very air, thick with the stench of decay and something indefinably ancient, felt almost...hungry. It seemed to actively absorb the essence of life, channeling it back into the pulsating black substance, fueling the unending cycle of monstrous birth and horrifying death.

Elias shivered, not just from the cold, but from a deeper, visceral revulsion. This was not merely a hostile environment; it was a malevolent one, a landscape designed to break the human spirit, to crush the very will to live. He remembered the cryptic warnings he'd found in the ancient texts – prophecies of a world where the line between life and death blurred, where the very boundaries of reality itself began to fray. This was it. This was the culmination of all those warnings, the physical manifestation of a nightmare he could never have imagined.

As he ventured deeper, the landscape grew even more grotesque. He passed through forests of petrified flesh, the trees resembling colossal, decaying corpses with gnarled, skeletal branches that seemed to writhe in the perpetual twilight. He saw rivers of viscous, black liquid flowing through the landscape, the liquid shimmering with the same unsettling bioluminescence, emitting a low, guttural hum that seemed to resonate deep within his bones. The creatures he encountered became increasingly monstrous, their forms a horrifying blend of organic and inorganic matter, their movements fluid yet strangely mechanical.

One such creature caught his eye - a massive, slug-like being that seemed to glide across the ground, leaving a trail of corrosive slime in its wake. Its back was a tapestry of pulsing, black growths, each one emitting a faint, rhythmic beat. He noticed that these growths were similar to the fungal structures he'd seen earlier, only far larger and more sinister. The slime trail it left behind seemed to interact with the black substance on the ground, causing it to pulsate with increased intensity. The creature appeared to be deliberately fertilizing the ground, somehow accelerating the grotesque growth of the environment.

He observed other creatures engaging in similar symbiotic relationships. A type of large, avian creature, its feathers as black as obsidian and tipped with bone-like spines, swooped down and pierced the pulsating flesh-trees with its beak, draining a viscous, black fluid. This fluid, he observed, was then regurgitated onto the black ground, further enriching it and fueling the growth of other grotesque flora. It was a horrifying dance of death and rebirth, a brutal cycle of predation and symbiotic co-existence. This place was a living testament to the fact that even in the darkest recesses of existence, life, in its most abhorrent form, found a way.

The air grew heavier, the oppressive atmosphere pressing down on him like a physical weight. He felt a growing sense of unease, a prickling on the back of his neck that told him he was being watched, observed by unseen eyes. The silence, broken only by the occasional rustling of the bone-trees and the low hum of the black rivers, was more terrifying than any shriek or roar could have been. It was the silence of a world devoid of hope, a world where every sound, every movement, was a testament to the relentless cycle of decay.

As he journeyed further, the twisted ecology became even more disturbing. He found evidence of a long-forgotten civilization, their ruins integrated into the grotesque landscape, their architecture a twisted mockery of natural forms. He discovered fragments of stone tablets inscribed with chilling symbols, detailing the origins of this nightmarish realm, the ancient pact made between the creatures and the dark forces that had shaped this world. The symbols hinted at rituals of sacrifice and unspeakable horrors, the creatures acting as both instruments and guardians of this abhorrent landscape. The civilization, it seemed, had become intertwined with the grotesque ecology, their bodies and their structures a part of this unending cycle of decay and renewal.

The horrifying truth, dawning upon him slowly, was that this wasn't simply a twisted ecosystem; it was a sentient entity, a monstrous being formed from the fusion of nature and nightmare. The black substance, the bone-dust, the creatures, the very landscape itself—all were parts of a single, monstrous organism, a living testament to the terrifying power of dark magic and forgotten gods. And Elias Thorne, a man haunted by his past, was now inextricably trapped within its horrifying embrace. His descent into darkness was far from over. The abyss was calling, and he was compelled to answer its summons. The fight for survival was only just beginning, a struggle not only against the monstrous creatures of this forsaken world but against the very fabric of reality itself. His resolve, hardened by the horrors he'd witnessed, steeled him for the trials ahead. He was now inextricably bound to this forsaken land, to fight a battle for his own survival, and, perhaps, for the survival of humanity itself. The true horror lay not just in what he saw, but in what he was becoming. The abyss was beckoning, and he was answering its call.

The wind, a mournful keening through the skeletal trees, whipped Elias's cloak around him, the fabric tasting of ash and decay. He stumbled onward, the landscape a relentless assault on his senses. The pulsating black substance, now familiar in its horror, seemed to writhe beneath his boots, a living carpet of nightmares. He'd lost track of time, days blurring into a nightmarish eternity. His hope, a flickering candle flame against a storm, threatened to extinguish itself at any moment. Then, he saw it – a flicker of movement amidst the grotesque tableau.

It wasn't one of the twisted, nightmarish creatures that stalked this cursed land. This was... different. A figure, hunched and frail, emerged from behind a particularly grotesque, bone-like protrusion of rock. The figure was clad in rags, the fabric stained with a deep, almost iridescent black, a color that seemed to absorb the already dim light. Its skin was pale, almost translucent, as if stretched taut over bone, and its eyes, deeply sunken, burned with an unnatural intensity. It was emaciated, its limbs thin as twigs, yet there was a strange resilience in its posture, a refusal to be broken.

Elias approached cautiously, weapon at the ready, his senses on high alert. The creature didn't flee, didn't attack. It simply watched him, its eyes, ancient and knowing, piercing through him. A low, rasping cough escaped its lips, a sound like dry leaves skittering across stone.

"Lost, are you?" the creature rasped, its voice a dry whisper that somehow cut through the oppressive silence. The language was strange, archaic, yet Elias somehow understood. It wasn't a learned language, but a primal understanding that resonated deep within his soul.

Elias, stunned by this unexpected encounter, lowered his weapon slightly. "I... I am lost," he admitted, his voice a rough echo in the desolate expanse. "I don't know how I got here, where I am..."

The creature nodded slowly, a gesture that seemed to take an immense effort. "This... is the Obsidian Waste," it whispered, its voice barely audible above the wind's mournful song. "A place forgotten by the gods, cursed by the ancients."

Elias felt a shiver run down his spine. He'd sensed the ancient malevolence of this place, the palpable presence of something beyond human comprehension. He hadn't realized, however, that the place itself was cursed.

"Who are you?" Elias asked, his voice trembling slightly.

"They call me Lyra," the creature replied. "A remnant... a survivor... of the Silent Ones."

The name, Silent Ones, stirred something within Elias, a faint echo in the recesses of his memory. It was a name whispered in forgotten texts, a civilization lost to time, spoken of in hushed tones as a people who had somehow defied the very gods.

Lyra, despite her frail appearance, possessed an uncanny knowledge of this hellish realm. She spoke of an ancient war, a conflict between powerful entities, gods and demons, that had shattered the world, leaving behind this desolate wasteland. She spoke of a gateway, a tear in reality, through which the horrors of this realm had spilled into the mortal world. She spoke of a prophecy, of a chosen one who would seal the gateway and prevent the ultimate apocalypse.

Elias listened, captivated by her words, his initial fear slowly giving way to a cautious hope. It was a desperate hope, clinging to a thread, yet it was there nonetheless. For the first time since his arrival in this nightmarish world, he felt a glimmer of possibility, a hint that escape, or at least a chance to fight back, might be possible.

Lyra, in her own twisted way, offered Elias comfort, a haven from the relentless horror of the Obsidian Waste. She led him to a hidden grotto, a small cave concealed behind a curtain of falling rocks. Inside, it was surprisingly dry and sheltered from the harsh elements. A small fire crackled in the center of the cavern, casting dancing shadows on the rough stone walls.

Lyra shared her meager rations, a few dried roots and berries gathered with painstaking effort from this barren landscape. The food tasted like ash and despair, yet Elias ate it gratefully, sustenance for his weary body and his dwindling hope.

She told him more about the Silent Ones, a civilization that had harnessed the power of ancient magic, a magic far older and more sinister than anything he had ever encountered. They had once thrived in this world, living in harmony with its darker aspects, until the war had shattered their civilization, leaving only a few scattered remnants.

Lyra was one of those remnants. She had lived in hiding for centuries, her knowledge of the ancient magic, the prophecies, and the true nature of the gateway, a burden she now wished to share with Elias.

She explained that the gateway was not simply a tear in reality, but a living entity, a monstrous being fueled by the dark magic that had ravaged this world. It was this being that created the Obsidian Waste, a nightmarish landscape designed to trap and consume those who dared to venture too close.

Lyra spoke of artifacts, powerful objects imbued with ancient magic, that could be used to seal the gateway, to push back the tide of darkness. These artifacts were scattered across the Waste, guarded by monstrous creatures born from the very essence of the darkness itself. Each artifact, she explained, possessed a piece of the ancient magic needed to perform the ritual. The risk was enormous, but so was the potential reward – the salvation of humanity.

Elias listened, absorbing every word, his mind racing. He was not a hero, nor was he a mage. He was a man haunted by his past, a man thrust into a nightmarish world beyond his comprehension. Yet, he was the only one who could potentially save humanity, as Lyra believed.

He saw the burden in Lyra's eyes, the weight of centuries of isolation, the knowledge of a lost civilization, and the desperate hope for a world reborn from the ashes of this horrifying abyss. He understood her desperation. He felt his own desperation mirror hers. They both clung to the same thread, a thread of hope in the face of unimaginable horror. The glimmer of hope, however faint, was stronger than it had been, a beacon in the encroaching darkness. The fight for survival wasn't just his own anymore; it was theirs, a shared burden and a shared destiny. The journey would be perilous, fraught with danger and unimaginable horrors, but with Lyra's knowledge and guidance, Elias felt a renewed strength surge within him. He would find the artifacts. He would seal the gateway. He would escape this nightmare. He had to. For Lyra, for humanity, and for himself. The descent into darkness had been brutal, but a path, however treacherous, had begun to appear, winding its way out of the abyss.

Lyra, her face etched with the weariness of ages, led Elias deeper into the heart of the forbidden world. The landscape shifted and twisted, a grotesque mockery of nature. Twisted trees clawed at the sky, their branches adorned with phosphorescent fungi that pulsed with a sickly, internal light. The air hung heavy with the stench of decay, a miasma that clung to the throat and choked the lungs. The ground beneath their feet was less earth and more a churning mass of obsidian, occasionally bubbling with the same pulsating black substance Elias had encountered before. It seemed to writhe and writhe and throb with a malevolent consciousness.

"This place... it feeds on fear," Lyra rasped, her voice barely a whisper above the incessant groan of the landscape. "It thrives on despair. The longer we stay, the more it weakens us, steals our will."

Elias nodded, his gaze fixed on the path ahead. He felt the chilling truth of her words seep into his bones. The very air seemed to press down on him, a suffocating blanket of dread. He'd already felt the creeping erosion of his own sanity, the gnawing doubt that whispered insidious lies in the darkest corners of his mind.

They moved in silence for a long while, the only sounds the crunching of their boots on the obsidian ground and the unsettling whisper of the wind. Then, Lyra stopped, her hand rising to point towards a colossal structure looming ahead, half-buried in the earth. It was a ruin, vast and imposing, its architecture alien and terrifying. Jagged obsidian spires pierced the perpetual twilight, and grotesque carvings, depicting scenes of unimaginable horror and ritualistic sacrifice, adorned its crumbling walls.

"The Citadel of Whispers," Lyra said, her voice barely audible. "The heart of it all."

As they approached, Elias felt a palpable shift in the atmosphere. The oppressive weight intensified, and the pulsating black substance seemed to writhe with even greater ferocity. The air thrummed with a low, guttural hum that vibrated deep within his bones.

The Citadel itself was a monument to a forgotten civilization, a testament to a power both ancient and malevolent. Its stones pulsed with a dark energy, and Elias could feel the weight of centuries of suffering emanating from its shattered walls. He saw glimpses of what appeared to be humanoid figures, but twisted and distorted into monstrous parodies of life, trapped within the very fabric of the structure, their screams echoing silently in the oppressive stillness.

Lyra led him through a crumbling archway, into a vast, cavernous chamber. The chamber was circular, its walls covered in intricate carvings that depicted a complex cosmology. These weren't simply decorative; they were maps, charts of a reality that existed beyond human comprehension. Elias recognized symbols that echoed those found on the artifact he'd discovered – the key that had opened this gateway to hell.

In the center of the chamber, a monolithic structure, seemingly made of the same pulsating black substance, dominated the space. It resembled an enormous heart, its surface writhing and pulsing with an internal light that shifted between shades of crimson and obsidian. It radiated a palpable sense of power, a malevolent energy that pressed against Elias's mind, attempting to penetrate his thoughts, to corrupt his very being.

"This...this is the source," Lyra whispered, her eyes wide with a mixture of fear and awe. "The heart of the gateway. It's been here for millennia, feeding off this world, fueling the incursions into our own."

As Lyra spoke, shadowy figures emerged from the darkness at the edges of the chamber. They moved with unnatural grace, their forms shifting and indistinct, their eyes burning with an unholy light. They were the guardians of the Citadel, creatures born from the darkness, beings of pure nightmare given form.

"They are the Harbingers," Lyra explained, her voice strained. "Servants of the Old Ones. They protect the gateway, ensuring the continued flow of power."

The Harbingers advanced, their movements silent but deadly. Their forms shifted and changed, morphing into grotesque parodies of human and animal forms, their features a blend of the horrific and the sublime. One moment, they resembled skeletal figures draped in tattered robes, the next, they were writhing masses of tentacles and claws. Their power was palpable, an aura of pure malevolence that chilled Elias to the bone.

But Lyra was prepared. She drew a wickedly curved blade from her cloak, its surface shimmering with an unearthly light. It was a weapon of ancient design, honed over centuries, imbued with a power that resonated with the very fabric of the forbidden world.

"They can't stand the light," Lyra said, her voice a low growl. "The light of our world. We need to reach the heart, sever its connection."

The battle was fierce and brutal. Elias fought alongside Lyra, his movements clumsy and desperate compared to her grace and deadly precision. He used the weapons he'd salvaged during his descent into this hellish world, each blow a desperate prayer. The Harbingers attacked with savage ferocity, their claws tearing at flesh and bone, their touch leaving behind a searing pain that spread through his body like wildfire.

Their numbers were vast, seemingly endless, but Lyra's skill and knowledge of their weaknesses kept them at bay. She moved like a wraith, her blade a blur of motion, cleaving through their ethereal forms with terrifying efficiency. Elias, though wounded and exhausted, held his ground, his determination fueled by the need to survive, to protect Lyra, and to seal the gateway.

As they fought their way towards the heart of the gateway, Lyra revealed fragments of the conspiracy. She spoke of ancient entities, beings of immense power that dwelled beyond the veil, their existence a perversion of creation itself. These Old Ones, as Lyra called them, had manipulated events for millennia, using the gateway to subtly influence the mortal world, slowly corrupting it, preparing it for their eventual arrival. The conspiracy extended far beyond this forbidden world, reaching into the highest echelons of power in Elias's own world. Powerful figures, influential leaders, and even religious institutions were unknowingly pawns in the Old Ones' grand scheme.

The Citadel of Whispers wasn't merely a gateway; it was a nexus, a point of convergence between worlds, where the influence of the Old Ones was most potent. The artifact Elias had found was only one piece of a much larger puzzle, a key to unlocking the gateway, but not the only key. The Old Ones had planted others throughout history, each one a potential doorway to their malevolent influence. The conspiracy was vast and intricate, a web of deceit and manipulation that spanned centuries, its tendrils wrapped around the very foundations of civilization.

As they finally reached the pulsating black heart, Lyra explained the final act. They had to sever the connection, destroy the heart. But it wouldn't be easy. The heart pulsed with a terrifying power, capable of obliterating them both in an instant.

Lyra explained that the artifact held a counter-energy, a force that could disrupt the Old Ones' control. They had to combine the energy of the artifact with the light of Elias's world - a potent counterpoint to the darkness of the forbidden realm.

The climax of their struggle was a harrowing dance between life and death, a desperate battle against unimaginable odds. Elias channeled the power of the artifact, his hands trembling as he focused his will, his mind battling against the crushing weight of the encroaching darkness, the insidious whispers of the Old Ones attempting to corrupt his resolve. The heart pulsed wildly, the ground shaking beneath their feet as Lyra positioned herself, preparing to deliver the final blow with her ancient blade. The fate of two worlds hung in the balance. The final confrontation was a symphony of screams, a clash of ancient energies, a fight for the very soul of existence itself.

The air crackled with a final, agonizing shriek as Lyra's blade plunged into the pulsating heart of the creature. The earth shuddered, a tremor that seemed to reach into Elias' very bones, before falling silent. A suffocating stillness descended, broken only by the ragged gasps of Elias himself and the slow, heavy breathing of Lyra. He felt the lingering echo of the battle, the raw power that had surged through him, leaving him drained, but alive. Or so he thought.

Lyra, her face pale and drawn, leaned against a jagged obsidian spire, her ancient blade dripping with a viscous, black ichor. Her usually sharp eyes were clouded with a strange, unsettling calm. "It is done," she whispered, her voice rasping, like dry leaves skittering across cracked earth. "The immediate threat is neutralized."

A wave of nausea washed over Elias. He felt the lingering effects of the battle, a deep exhaustion that settled in his bones. The power of the artifact throbbed faintly within him, a dull ache beneath his ribs. He glanced at the lifeless form of the creature – a grotesque parody of life, its flesh now a blackened char, its eyes staring vacantly into the void. He shuddered. This victory felt hollow, almost...wrong.

Lyra's sudden stillness, the unsettling calm that had replaced her usual fierce determination, unsettled him. She was acting strangely. As if she was hiding something.

"Lyra," Elias began, his voice hoarse, "are you alright?"

She didn't answer immediately. Her gaze drifted away, towards the perpetually twilight sky, a sky perpetually stained with the colours of a dying sunset. Her eyes, usually filled with a fiery intensity, were now dulled, as if the light within them had been extinguished. Then, slowly, she turned to him, a flicker of something cold and calculating in her eyes. Something that wasn't sorrow, not remorse, but something far colder – betrayal.

"Perhaps 'alright' is not the appropriate word, Elias," she said, her voice devoid of emotion. "I am... satisfied."

Her words hung in the air, heavy and ominous, the chilling precursor to the true horror that was about to unfold. The satisfaction she spoke of wasn't the simple satisfaction of a battle won; it was a chilling, almost predatory satisfaction that sent a shiver down Elias's spine.

Before Elias could question her further, a change swept over Lyra. Her skin shimmered, taking on an unnatural, oily sheen. Her eyes, previously dull, now blazed with an incandescent, otherworldly light. Her movements, once fluid and graceful, became jerky and unnatural, as if her body were being controlled by an unseen force.

"You were a useful tool, Elias Thorne," she hissed, her voice now a guttural rasp, barely human. "But your usefulness is at an end."

The transformation was complete. Lyra, the warrior who had fought beside him, who had guided him through this infernal landscape, was gone, replaced by something... else. Something ancient, something wicked, something undeniably malevolent. The artifact pulsed violently against his chest, reacting to the change in Lyra with a frightening intensity.

He stumbled back, his mind reeling from the sudden betrayal. The ground seemed to tilt beneath his feet, the grotesque landscape swirling around him in a dizzying kaleidoscope of shadows and distorted forms. He was surrounded by the oppressive silence of the forbidden world, the chilling quiet before a storm, and the storm was Lyra. She was now the storm.

"The Old Ones... they didn't control me," she said, the voice of the Old Ones – ancient, rasping, and utterly alien – resonating now from her. "I... I served them willingly."

A wave of nausea washed over Elias, as the horrifying truth revealed itself. The whispers of the Old Ones he had fought so hard to resist, had found a home in Lyra. The seemingly selfless warrior, the guiding light in his descent into darkness, was merely their pawn, their willing vessel. He had trusted her, relied on her, and now she was turning against him, more dangerous than any of the monstrous creatures he had encountered thus far.

Her body twisted in ways that defied human anatomy. Limbs elongated, contorted, and reformed into something vaguely insectoid, yet strangely elegant. The change, grotesque as it was, was beautiful in a terrifying sort of way, a testament to the terrifying power of the ancient entities she now served.

She lunged at him, her movements swift and deadly, her newly formed limbs a blur of motion. Elias barely had time to react, his body moving on pure instinct, as the artifact's power coursed through his veins. He parried her attack, the clash of his makeshift weapon against her transformed limbs echoing in the unsettling stillness of the forbidden world.

The battle was brutal, a horrifying dance of death played out in the heart of the nightmare realm. Elias, despite his exhaustion, fought with a desperate ferocity, fueled by betrayal and a primal instinct to survive. He felt the corrupting influence of the Old Ones washing over him, tempting him to yield, to join their ranks, to give in to the overwhelming power they offered. But the memory of his past, the promise of a future he might yet salvage, fueled his resistance.

Lyra fought with a cold precision, her movements inhuman, her strength augmented by the ancient energies that flowed through her. She was stronger than before, faster, more lethal. Each blow landed with the force of a battering ram, each strike infused with the chilling power of the Old Ones. His every parry was a desperate gamble against the abyss.

The battle raged for what felt like an eternity, each strike a desperate struggle against overwhelming odds. Elias, fuelled by adrenaline and sheer will, fought with the fury of a cornered animal. Yet, with every parry, with every desperate dodge, he felt the darkness encroaching upon him, the insidious whispers of the Old Ones growing stronger, their promises of power, of oblivion, becoming almost irresistible.

He stumbled, his legs giving way beneath the onslaught of her attacks. He fell to his knees, his breath ragged, his body screaming in protest. Lyra loomed over him, her face, or what was left of it, contorted in a predatory grin, and he saw a reflection of his own despair in her unnervingly bright eyes. The darkness, the irresistible lure of the Old Ones' power, beckoned him, whispering promises of power and an end to his suffering. He was moments away from succumbing to their seductive influence. Moments away from becoming one of them.

But then, a flicker of defiance, a stubborn ember of his humanity ignited within him, refusing to be extinguished. The memory

of his family, his friends, his past, all the things
he still fought to protect, burned brighter than
the seductive darkness. He refused to give in.

He reached for the artifact, gripping it
with all his might, willing it to react, to help
him, to find a way to fight back, to escape this
nightmare he had stumbled into. With a final,
desperate surge of willpower, he pushed back
against the corrupting influence of the Old
Ones and focused his will upon the artifact, its
power surging through him once more, in a
wave stronger and more focused than before.
This was no longer a fight for survival. This
was a fight for his soul.

Chapter 3:

Echoes of the Past

The rasping breath hitched in his throat, a sound swallowed by the suffocating darkness. Elias Thorne awoke not to the gentle caress of dawn, but to the brutal, clawing grip of a memory. It wasn't a memory so much as a visceral experience, a sensory overload that threatened to shatter his sanity. He was a child again, no older than seven, huddled beneath the rotting floorboards of a derelict house, the stench of mildew and decay clinging to the air like a shroud. The rhythmic thump-thump-thump of something large and unseen vibrated through the floor, a relentless heartbeat that echoed in the marrow of his bones. Terror, primal and unyielding, constricted his chest.

The image flickered, shifting and reforming like a disturbed reflection in murky water. The house was different now, its decaying timbers replaced by obsidian spires that clawed at a bruised, blood-red sky. The thumping sound intensified, evolving into a guttural roar that seemed to tear the very fabric of reality. He saw it then, a silhouette of grotesque majesty against the crimson horizon: a colossal creature, a being of nightmare made flesh, its form shifting and writhing, a tapestry woven from shadow and something far more sinister.

The memory, or hallucination, intensified, the creature's shadow engulfing him, its presence radiating a palpable sense of dread. Elias felt a cold, clammy touch upon his arm, a sensation that transcended physical contact, a direct assault on his soul. He cried out, a wordless scream of terror that was lost in the echoing void of the memory. Then, just as suddenly as it had begun, the vision dissolved, leaving him gasping for air in the relative safety of his present surroundings.

Sweat slicked his skin, his heart hammering against his ribs like a trapped bird. He sat up in the rough-hewn bed, the coarse fabric scratching against his skin, a stark contrast to the chilling reality of the vision. He ran a hand through his matted hair, the gesture a desperate attempt to anchor himself in the present. The survivor, the woman he'd met in the forbidden world, had warned him that his past held the key to understanding this terrifying realm, but Elias hadn't anticipated the brutality of the revelation.

The artifact, the source of his descent into this nightmarish landscape, pulsed faintly beneath his shirt. Its surface, cold and smooth to the touch, seemed to thrum with a sinister energy, a resonance that mirrored the horrifying images that still danced behind his closed eyelids. He traced the intricate carvings on its surface, symbols that seemed both ancient and alien, hinting at a forgotten language, a lost history. He felt a connection to it, a disturbing kinship that both frightened and intrigued him.

He thought back to the cryptic words the woman had spoken, her voice a haunting echo in the chambers of his mind. "The blood of the ancients flows in your veins, Elias Thorne. You are the key, and the lock, and the terrible price to be paid." Her words, delivered with a chilling certainty, now felt heavier, pregnant with a significance he hadn't grasped before.

He remembered another fragment, a fleeting image from his childhood: a shadowy figure, cloaked in darkness, whispering promises of power and secrets beyond comprehension. The figure's face was obscured, but he could still feel the unsettling warmth of its presence, a disturbing comfort that he could not explain. This figure, he now suspected, was connected to the artifact, to the forbidden world, and to the horrifying creature that haunted his dreams.

His recollections weren't confined to frightening images; there were fleeting moments of peace amidst the chaos. He remembered a sun-drenched meadow, the scent of wildflowers filling the air, the laughter of children echoing through the trees. It was a stark contrast to the nightmarish landscapes he'd witnessed in the forbidden world. Yet, even these peaceful memories felt tainted, edged with a subtle dissonance, a hint of something wrong, something lurking just beneath the surface.

The realization struck him with the force of a physical blow: his memories were fragmented, distorted, a puzzle with missing pieces. They were not simply memories; they were fragments of a larger narrative, a narrative that intertwined his past with the terrifying realities of the forbidden world. The artifact, he now understood, was not just a gateway; it was a conduit, a connection to his own suppressed history. It was a key, not only to unlocking the secrets of the forbidden world but to unlocking the darkest corners of his own mind.

He recalled the survivor's words again, the chilling detail of the ancient civilization that once thrived in this realm. A civilization that had mastered powers beyond human comprehension, a civilization that had ultimately fallen prey to the very darkness it sought to control. The images flashed before his eyes: towering cities carved from living rock, intricate machinery humming with an unsettling energy, and the faces of people, both human and not quite human, etched with a mixture of fear and awe.

Their demise, the survivor had explained, was not a simple conquest, but a slow, agonizing corruption. The darkness that had consumed this civilization had burrowed its way into their very being, twisting their bodies and minds, until they were something monstrous, something other. The thought sent a chill down his spine, a profound sense of dread that sunk deep into his soul. He felt a strange, symbiotic connection with these forgotten people, a sense of shared fate that was as terrifying as it was intriguing.

He had to understand more. He had to unravel the mystery of his own past, to understand the connection between his childhood memories, the artifact, and the horrifying creatures that roamed the forbidden world. The weight of this task pressed upon him, heavy and suffocating. It was not merely a quest for survival; it was a quest for self-discovery, a confrontation with the darkest aspects of his own being.

As the sun began to climb, painting the sky with hues of bruised purple and blood orange, Elias rose from his bed. He felt the artifact's pulse against his skin, a constant reminder of the terrifying power he now held in his hands. The echoes of his past, once fragmented and indistinct, were now coalescing, forming a chilling narrative that threatened to consume him entirely. The journey ahead promised to be treacherous, filled with unimaginable horrors and impossible choices. But Elias Thorne, haunted by the whispers of his past, was determined to face whatever lay ahead. He was no longer just a man haunted by his past; he was a man driven by it, a man on a desperate quest to uncover the truth, even if that truth were to shatter him completely. His destiny, it seemed, was inextricably linked to the fate of the forbidden world and the terrifying secrets it held. The price of knowledge, he knew, would be paid in blood, sweat, and perhaps even his own soul. And yet, he would pay it. He had to.

The old woman, her face a roadmap of wrinkles etched by time and hardship, coughed, a rattling sound like dry leaves skittering across cobblestones. Her eyes, though clouded with age, held a spark of something ancient, something that resonated with the unsettling power Elias felt emanating from the artifact clutched in his hand. She spoke in a low, gravelly voice, her words laced with the weight of centuries.

"They called themselves the Kryll," she rasped, her voice barely audible above the drip, drip, drip of water echoing from unseen depths. "Masters of shadow and bone, weavers of nightmares. They were... different. Not quite human, not quite... anything else." She paused, her breath hitching in her chest, the effort of speaking clearly visible in the tremor of her frail hands.

Elias leaned closer, his attention rapt. He knew this was the information he had been seeking, the key to understanding this nightmarish realm and his own unsettling connection to it. "Different how?" he asked, his voice a low murmur in the cavernous space.

"Their very essence was... twisted," she whispered, her gaze drifting to some unseen point in the darkness. "They drew power from the shadows, from the fears and despair of others. They thrived on suffering, on the slow, agonizing decay of the soul. Their cities were built not of stone or wood, but of solidified nightmares, of twisted bone and echoing whispers. Imagine, if you will, a city sculpted from the very essence of dread, each building a monument to despair, each street a pathway to madness."

He shuddered, the image vivid and horrifying. He'd already glimpsed glimpses of this world's twisted beauty, its grotesque artistry, in the monstrous creatures that lurked in its shadowy corners. This was a world born of darkness, of nightmares given form.

"They weren't born here," the woman continued, her voice regaining some of its strength. "They came from... beyond. From a place that exists only in the deepest recesses of the mind, a place where reality warps and the very fabric of existence frays." She shuddered, as if recalling something deeply unpleasant. "They brought with them a power that corrupted everything it touched, twisting the very land itself into a reflection of their twisted souls."

She described a civilization of horrifying beauty, their architecture a grotesque mockery of human design. Buildings clawed at the sky, their skeletal frames interwoven with veins of obsidian and pulsating, fleshy growths. Towers, fashioned from colossal bone structures, reached towards a sky choked with perpetual twilight. The ground itself was unsettling – a shifting landscape of cracked earth, punctuated by pools of viscous, black ichor that hissed and bubbled ominously. The air itself felt thick with a palpable sense of dread, a miasma of fear and despair that seemed to seep into Elias's very bones.

The Kryll, she explained, were not a unified people. They were fractured into warring factions, each vying for dominance, each employing horrifying rituals and twisted magics. They engaged in grotesque sacrifices, draining the life force from their victims to fuel their dark power. The landscape was scarred

with the remnants of their brutal conflicts –
shattered remnants of their obsidian cities,
battlefields littered with the bleached bones of
their victims.

Their demise, she revealed, was as
horrifying as their existence. It wasn't a swift
end, but a slow, agonizing decline brought
about by their own insatiable hunger for power.
Their constant warring, their reckless
consumption of life-force, eventually led to a
catastrophic imbalance in the very fabric of this
realm. The land itself rebelled, erupting in a
cataclysmic upheaval of shadow and fire. The
earth itself seemed to reject them, consuming
their cities, swallowing them whole.

"Their power, their very essence, was
bound to this place," the woman croaked, her
voice a mere whisper. "But when they fell, that
power... it fractured. It seeped into the land,
into the creatures, into everything. That's what
you feel, that's what you're connected to."

Elias felt a chill crawl down his spine.
The artifact in his hand pulsed, a rhythmic beat
mirroring the ancient woman's words. He
understood now; the horror he felt, the
terrifying visions, the connection to this

desolate realm – it was all linked to the Kryll, to their horrific legacy. He was somehow intertwined with their history, a thread in the tapestry of their nightmare, a potential key to their ultimate destruction or perhaps, a vessel for their horrific rebirth.

The old woman continued, her voice a frail thread against the oppressive silence. "They weren't all evil," she whispered, a surprising note of sadness in her tone. "Some... some sought to escape their own dark fate. They knew the consequences of their actions, the inevitable destruction they were bringing upon themselves. They tried to warn others, to seal away their power before it consumed everything."

She described a desperate attempt by a faction of the Kryll to contain their destructive magic, a final, desperate act of self-preservation. They had created a series of intricate wards, powerful enchantments woven into the very fabric of the land, designed to trap and contain the essence of their civilization. These wards, however, were not meant to be permanent. They were a temporary solution, a desperate measure to buy time, a fragile barrier against the encroaching darkness.

The artifact, she revealed, was a key component of these wards. It held a fragment of their power, a conduit to their corrupted magic, capable of both unleashing their destructive essence or sealing it away forever. This revelation sent a fresh wave of dread through Elias. He held in his hand not just a powerful artifact, but a weapon of unimaginable potential, capable of both creating untold destruction and saving this forsaken world from its horrific past.

The weight of this responsibility was almost unbearable. The woman's story had revealed a civilization driven by monstrous desires, a people who had created a world born from their own nightmares. But it also revealed a flicker of hope, a desperate attempt at redemption, a final, tragic effort to prevent their catastrophic downfall. Now, Elias was caught in the middle, burdened with the responsibility to choose, to decide whether to use the power of the artifact to undo the horrors of the Kryll, or to unleash the dark legacy they had left behind.

The silence that followed was oppressive, punctuated only by the woman's ragged breathing. The implications of her words hung heavy in the air, a suffocating blanket of dread and responsibility. Elias felt the artifact thrumming against his skin, a constant, unsettling reminder of the power he now held, the power that could determine the fate of this world, and perhaps, even his own. The choices that lay ahead were terrifying, the consequences unimaginable. But one thing was clear: his journey had just begun, and the path ahead was paved with the shattered remnants of a forgotten civilization, and the chilling echoes of their demise.

The old woman, her voice strained, gave Elias one last piece of crucial information. Hidden deep within the heart of the Kryll's ruined capital, a place they called 'The Obsidian Heart,' lay the final piece of the warding system. It was a powerful artifact, even more potent than the one Elias possessed, capable of permanently sealing away the Kryll's corrupted essence. Finding it, however, would be a treacherous and perilous undertaking. The city was a maze of twisted architecture, haunted by remnants of the Kryll's twisted creations, guarded by grotesque creatures born from their nightmares. The journey promised to be fraught with peril, but Elias knew he had no choice. His fate, and the fate of this world, hung in the balance.

He thanked the old woman, a deep bow expressing his gratitude for her insight. He left her in the darkness, her frail form barely visible in the gloom, and began his trek to the Obsidian Heart, carrying the weight of the Kryll's legacy, the burden of their dark history, and the responsibility of shaping the future of this terrifying world. He moved cautiously, the artifact pulsing in his hand, a constant reminder of the terrible power he possessed, the power that could rewrite the very essence of this nightmarish realm. The echoes of the Kryll, their terrifying whispers and haunting memories, clung to him like a shroud, urging him onward, pushing him towards a destiny he was only beginning to understand. The path ahead was treacherous, the dangers unimaginable, but Elias Thorne, haunted by his own cryptic past and driven by the weight of responsibility, would not turn back. He would face the Obsidian Heart, and the unimaginable horrors that lay within. He would confront the ghosts of the Kryll, and decide the fate of a world teetering on the brink of oblivion.

The path to the Obsidian Heart was a descent into a hellscape. Jagged obsidian spires clawed at the bruised, twilight sky, their surfaces slick with a viscous, black ichor that dripped and hissed like a malevolent rain. The air itself was thick with the stench of decay – a miasma of sulfur, burnt flesh, and something indescribably ancient and foul. Each step Elias took echoed with a hollow resonance, the sound bouncing off the unnatural formations as if the very landscape itself were a grotesque, echoing tomb.

The artifact, a tarnished silver locket shaped like a snarling skull, throbbed against his skin, its cold metal a stark contrast to the sweat beading on his brow. He felt its power grow with each passing moment, a burgeoning energy that both exhilarated and terrified him. It wasn't just a physical sensation; it was a psychic assault, a torrent of images and emotions flooding his mind – visions of unspeakable rituals, of civilizations consumed by darkness, of beings born from nightmare itself.

He fought to maintain control, his will a fragile dam against a raging torrent. The Kryll's whispers, once faint echoes, now roared in his ears, a chorus of tormented voices vying for dominance. They spoke of power, of dominion, of the terrifying potential held within the locket. They urged him to embrace the darkness, to become one with the horrifying forces they had once served.

He stumbled, the ground beneath his feet shifting like quicksand. He caught himself, the locket's pulsing rhythm steadying his breath. He focused on the present, on the treacherous path, on the looming presence of the Obsidian Heart, pushing back against the tide of madness threatening to engulf him. The whispers intensified, weaving themselves into the fabric of his thoughts, twisting his memories, trying to break his resolve. He saw fleeting glimpses of his own past – a shadowed figure, a chilling scream, a feeling of profound loss that had haunted him since childhood. The Kryll were trying to connect their dark history with his own, creating a powerful link between their doom and his destiny.

He pressed on, ignoring the insidious voices, determined to reach his destination. He knew that the locket was not merely a key; it was a conduit, a focus for the terrible energy that pulsed through this forsaken realm. The old woman's words echoed in his mind: "The Obsidian Heart holds the gateway. The locket...it controls the flow. But beware, the power is a double-edged sword. It can seal the gateway, or it can unleash a hell far beyond your comprehension."

As he approached the Obsidian Heart, the visions became more frequent, more vivid. He saw towering figures, cloaked in shadows, performing grotesque sacrifices beneath a blood-red moon. He witnessed the annihilation of entire civilizations, the landscapes consumed by a creeping darkness, the screams of the dying echoing through eternity. The Kryll's reign of terror was laid bare before him, a horrifying spectacle of power and depravity. They were not merely cruel; they were architects of nightmare, their dominion fueled by an insatiable hunger for suffering. They had used the artifact to unleash their monstrous energies, corrupting this realm into a reflection of their own twisted souls. And he now understood that this locket wasn't just a key; it was the very heart of their power.

The Obsidian Heart itself was a terrifying sight. It wasn't a literal heart, but a colossal obsidian monolith, pulsating with an internal light that seemed to writhe and shift like some monstrous entity trapped within.

Runes, ancient and indecipherable, were etched into its surface, their power radiating outward in waves of chilling energy. The ground around it was scorched, scarred by the impact of some unimaginable cataclysm. The air crackled with power, the silence broken only by the low, guttural growls emanating from the Heart itself.

As he drew closer, the Kryll's whispers intensified, morphing into a cacophony of voices that seemed to claw at his sanity. They offered him power, dominion over this nightmarish realm. They promised him vengeance, the ability to rewrite his own history, to erase the pain and loss that had haunted him for so long. They painted a seductive picture of control, of absolute power, where his every whim would become reality, where his past traumas would become sources of strength.

But Elias resisted. He clutched the locket tighter, the cold metal grounding him in the face of overwhelming temptation. He remembered the old woman's warning, the potential for devastation. He saw in his mind's eye not only the suffering of the Kryll, but also the potential suffering of humanity – a world

devoured by the darkness if the gateway
remained open.

He reached out, his hand trembling,
towards the Obsidian Heart. The artifact
pulsed in response, the snarling skull seeming
to mirror his own internal struggle. He focused
on his intention – to seal the gateway, to
protect humanity from the horrors that lay
beyond. He channeled his fear, his pain, his
resolve into the locket, infusing it with his own
will.

The air crackled, the ground trembled.
The Obsidian Heart resonated with a violent
energy, the runes glowing with an infernal
light. Elias felt a wave of power wash over him,
threatening to overwhelm him. He fought back,
his will hardening, his determination
unwavering. He pushed the Kryll's whispers
back, silencing their insidious temptations.

He concentrated on the locket,
visualizing the gateway closing, the darkness
receding. He poured all his remaining strength
into the artifact, and at that moment, he felt a
connection, a powerful link to the Obsidian
Heart. The monstrous energy within began to
coalesce, to obey his command. The runes

pulsed, their infernal glow dimming as if in response to his will. He felt a searing pain, as if his very soul were being ripped apart. But he held on, driven by the hope of salvation.

Slowly, agonizingly, the Obsidian Heart's pulsating light began to fade. The grotesque energy within seemed to recede, the growls diminishing to a low hum. The oppressive atmosphere began to lift, the stench of decay gradually replaced by a chilling, yet strangely comforting silence. The runes on the monolith went dark, their malevolent power extinguished. The gateway was closing.

Exhausted, barely conscious, Elias collapsed to his knees. The locket lay inert in his hand, its power spent, its purpose fulfilled. The echoes of the Kryll's whispers were gone, replaced by a profound emptiness. The horrors he'd witnessed, the temptations he'd resisted, the power he'd wielded – it all left him drained, yet strangely liberated. He had faced the darkness and emerged, not unscathed, but victorious. He had sealed the gateway, saving humanity from a fate far worse than oblivion. But the echoes of the past, both his own and that of the Kryll, remained, a chilling reminder of the terrifying power he had confronted, and the horrifying truth he now possessed. The battle was over, but the war, he knew, was far from won.

The obsidian landscape, once a terrifying maelstrom of monstrous entities and arcane power, now lay still, shrouded in an unnatural quiet. The air, though still heavy with the stench of decay, felt less oppressive, the oppressive weight of the Kryll's presence lifted. But the silence was worse, a suffocating blanket that amplified the turmoil within Elias. The victory felt hollow, a pyrrhic triumph earned at a cost he was only beginning to understand.

He sat amidst the jagged obsidian spires, the locket, its surface now dulled and cold, lying forgotten in his palm. The echoes of the Kryll's whispers, once a cacophony of maddening promises and terrifying threats, were gone, leaving behind a vacuum filled with the reverberations of his own tormented past. Memories, long suppressed, clawed their way to the surface, their sharp edges tearing at the fragile fabric of his sanity.

He remembered the flickering gaslight of his childhood home, the chilling silence that followed his father's screams, the suffocating fear that clung to him like a shroud. He saw his mother's haunted eyes, her whispered pleas that were ultimately swallowed by the abyss of his father's madness. The asylum, its cold, sterile walls, the metallic tang of fear and despair, the hollow echoing of his own screams – it all came flooding back, a torrent of pain and regret.

The Kryll had fed on his fear, his vulnerability, twisting his anxieties into weapons against him. They had shown him visions, glimpses of futures warped by his own insecurities, futures where his past consumed him, a self-fulfilling prophecy of self-destruction. He'd faced their monstrous forms, battled their insidious whispers, but the most terrifying battle was yet to come: the confrontation with the demons that resided within.

The obsidian shards beneath him seemed to mirror the fractured pieces of his soul. He felt the weight of his past, a physical burden that crushed him, each memory a fresh wound that refused to heal. The Kryll's power, although banished, had left an insidious residue, a psychic scar that throbbed with a dark, persistent energy. He was no longer just haunted; he was possessed, not by external forces, but by the ghosts of his own making.

He closed his eyes, attempting to block out the relentless assault of memories. But the darkness behind his eyelids was far more terrifying than any external horror. He saw his father's face, contorted in rage, his eyes burning with an unnatural fire. He heard the chilling laughter of the asylum's inmates, their voices weaving together in a terrifying chorus. He felt the icy grip of isolation, the utter loneliness that had defined his childhood and haunted him into adulthood.

The Kryll had shown him the potential for darkness within him, the capacity for cruelty and despair that lay dormant, waiting to be unleashed. They had tempted him with power, with the promise of vengeance against those who had wronged him. And he'd resisted, choosing to seal the gateway instead of succumbing to the seductive whispers of his inner demons. Yet, the temptation remained, a lingering echo of their dark promises. Was his resistance merely a testament to his resilience or a fragile facade masking a deeper, darker truth?

Days bled into nights. Elias remained amidst the obsidian ruins, the landscape a reflection of his internal struggle. The silence was broken only by the mournful cry of unseen birds, the wind whispering secrets through the jagged spires, and the ceaseless turmoil within his own mind. He ate little, slept less, his body a vessel ravaged by physical and mental exhaustion. He felt the creeping tendrils of madness threatening to engulf him, to shatter what remained of his sanity.

He tried to find solace in the task he'd accomplished, the salvation of humanity. But the scale of his victory felt inconsequential against the vastness of his personal torment. The Kryll were defeated, but their influence lingered, a dark stain on his soul. He'd faced the monsters of the forbidden world, but the true monsters, the ones he'd always carried within, were far more dangerous.

He began to dig, driven by an instinct he didn't understand, his hands tearing at the obsidian earth, his fingers bleeding. He wasn't searching for anything tangible; he was searching for release, for a way to purge the memories, to exorcise the demons that had consumed him. He dug until his hands were raw and bleeding, until his body ached, until he collapsed, his body shuddering with exhaustion and the lingering tremors of a trauma he had only just begun to confront.

In his delirium, he saw faces – not just the faces of his tormented past, but the faces of the Kryll, their eyes burning with a malevolent light, their whispers transforming into taunts. They were mocking his victory, reminding him that he had merely banished them, not defeated them. They were laughing, a chilling, guttural sound that echoed the laughter of the asylum inmates, the laughter of his own shattered psyche.

He found a small, smooth stone, dark grey, almost black. As he held it, a vision flared in his mind: a memory, not his own, but a memory from the Kryll. He saw a vast, starless void, and within it, a swirling vortex of black energy. He saw faces, countless faces, all twisted in agony, their screams echoing through the void. It was the primordial darkness, the source of the Kryll's power, the wellspring of their nightmares. He understood then that the Kryll were not merely creatures of this forbidden world; they were born of it, manifestations of the cosmic horror that lay at the heart of existence.

The vision shattered, leaving him gasping for breath, his heart pounding like a war drum. He was close, he realized; close to understanding the true nature of the threat, the nature of the darkness that he'd confronted and, perhaps, a way to truly vanquish it. It wasn't enough to seal a gateway; he needed to understand the roots of the darkness, to confront the source of the evil that threatened to consume all of existence.

But even as this realization dawned, a chilling certainty washed over him. The Kryll were gone, but their essence, their darkness, remained. He carried it within him, a constant, gnawing reminder of the horrors he'd witnessed, the battles he'd fought, and the demons he still had to conquer. His journey wasn't over. It had only just begun. The fight for his own sanity, the fight against his inner demons, was a battle that would define the rest of his existence. He was changed, irrevocably scarred, yet he stood, a broken man, staring into the abyss and seeing a reflection of his own soul staring back. The battle against the external horrors was won, but the war within had just begun, and it promised to be far more brutal.

The obsidian shards crunched under Elias's boots, a morbid counterpoint to the unsettling quiet. The Kryll's absence was a wound as gaping as the chasm that had swallowed their monstrous legions. He ran a hand across his face, feeling the phantom ache of a blow that had nearly shattered his skull, a testament to the brutal battle just concluded. The victory felt like ashes in his mouth, bitter and unsatisfying. He had sealed the gateway, or so he believed, but the price was etched into his very being – a chilling certainty that the war was far from over.

His gaze drifted to the artifact, the grotesque, pulsating heart of the Kryll, now inert, its power seemingly drained. It lay nestled within a fractured piece of the obsidian, a chilling memento of the nightmare he had survived. He'd initially intended to destroy it, to obliterate any vestige of the Kryll's foul existence, but a cold, calculating voice, born from the depths of his own exhaustion and trauma, whispered a different course.

The Kryll were gone, but the knowledge, the understanding of their power, their terrifying capabilities, remained. He, Elias Thorne, was now a repository of that knowledge, a living testament to their depravity. And this terrifying understanding presented him with a choice, a crucial decision that resonated with the weight of the world itself. He could destroy the artifact, ensuring that no one else would ever unlock the gateway to the forbidden realms. Or he could retain it, study it, attempt to unravel the mysteries it held, hoping to prevent future incursions, to understand the very nature of the darkness he had confronted.

The thought of destroying it was tempting, a siren song of relief and escape. It would mean a return to relative normalcy, to a life devoid of the constant threat of monstrous entities and arcane horrors. But the whisper of his own ambition, a perverse echo of the insatiable hunger he'd seen in the Kryll themselves, kept him rooted to the spot. He yearned for answers, a desperate craving to understand the nature of this abyss he had glimpsed, the secrets of a forgotten world that could consume reality itself.

The weight of the decision pressed upon him, a physical burden that threatened to crush him under its immense pressure. He was no hero, no chosen one destined to save the world. He was a man broken by trauma, scarred by his past, and now burdened with a power he barely understood. Yet, the thought of leaving the world vulnerable to the Kryll's return, of leaving the potential for such devastation to fester and grow, was a burden far heavier than the artifact itself.

Days bled into nights, each sunrise offering little respite from the gnawing uncertainty. Elias remained by the chasm, the silence broken only by the wind whispering through the jagged obsidian. He examined the artifact meticulously, its surface cold and unyielding, radiating a faint, unsettling warmth that seemed to pulse in time with his own erratic heartbeat. He studied its intricate patterns, the grotesque carvings that seemed to writhe and shift even as he looked upon them. He even tried to communicate with it, to glean whatever knowledge it might yield. He whispered questions into its cold stillness, questions about the Kryll, about the forbidden realms, about the nature of the darkness that clung to him like a shroud.

The answers, when they came, were fragmented, disturbing visions that danced behind his eyelids - fleeting glimpses of forgotten rituals, of monstrous births and unholy unions, of a civilization that had dabbled in powers beyond human comprehension. He saw cities built of bone, rivers of blood, skies stained with the unholy glow of forbidden magics. He felt the chilling presence of entities beyond human understanding, their malevolent thoughts scraping at the edges of his sanity. The visions were nightmarish, horrifying, yet they were also pieces of a puzzle, fragments of a truth he desperately needed to piece together.

His nights were filled with these waking nightmares, his days with the painstaking examination of the artifact. The once-sharp edges of his sanity began to dull, the lines between reality and the visions blurring. He could feel the darkness, the legacy of the Kryll, seeping into his very soul, twisting his thoughts, corrupting his judgment. Yet, he pressed on, driven by a desperate need to understand, to control the monstrous power he had unwittingly acquired.

He found himself studying ancient texts, dusty tomes forgotten in the libraries of forgotten empires. He sought out whispers of forgotten languages, archaic symbols that hinted at the rituals and ceremonies of the Kryll. He learned of alliances forged in darkness, of ancient pacts made with entities beyond comprehension. He pieced together the fragmented lore, drawing parallels between the Kryll and other forgotten horrors, uncovering a terrifying tapestry of malevolence that stretched across millennia.

His research was not without its perils. The very act of uncovering this knowledge seemed to attract attention, shadowy figures flitting at the periphery of his awareness, their motives as inscrutable as their identities. He sensed them watching him, waiting, their presence a constant prickle at the back of his neck, a chilling reminder that he was not alone in his quest. He knew they were after the artifact, after the power it represented, and he began to realize that his decision to keep it was not just a gamble on preventing the future, but a perilous game with forces far more ancient and powerful than himself.

But the cost was immense. The visions grew more frequent, more vivid, leaving him drained and haunted. He started seeing the faces of the Kryll in the mundane, their grotesque forms merging with the faces of the people he passed on the streets. The stench of decay, the cloying scent of death and putrefaction, followed him everywhere, an ever-present reminder of the hellish landscape he had escaped.

His sleep was fitful, punctuated by night terrors that sent him screaming into the cold night air, his dreams filled with the echoing cries of the Kryll, their desperate pleas for power, their insatiable hunger. He was walking a razor's edge, balancing precariously between sanity and utter madness, his body and mind weary from the relentless strain of his mission.

Yet, despite the horror, despite the mounting madness, despite the knowledge that he was playing a game with forces far beyond his comprehension, Elias refused to falter. The fate of the world, as far as he could understand, rested on his shoulders, on his ability to comprehend and control the power of the artifact, to use the knowledge he was gaining against the very darkness that threatened to consume him. His decision was made, and now he would pay the price. The war within had begun, and it was far more terrifying than any battle he had ever faced in the forbidden realms. The weight of the world pressed down on him, but he would not yield. He would face the darkness, even if it meant losing himself in the process.

Chapter 4:

The Monstrous Alliance

The air hung thick and cloying, a miasma of decay and something indescribably ancient. Elias, his lungs burning with the acrid stench, stumbled through a landscape that defied description. Twisted, skeletal trees clawed at the bruised, perpetually twilight sky, their branches adorned with phosphorescent fungi that pulsed with an unnerving, internal light. The ground beneath his feet was a treacherous mosaic of cracked earth and glistening, viscous puddles that seemed to writhe with unseen life.

He'd been separated from the survivor, Theron, during their desperate flight from the monstrous entity they'd only narrowly escaped. Theron, with his gaunt frame and eyes that held the wisdom – and the weariness – of centuries, had proven to be a surprisingly effective guide through this hellscape. But their escape had been chaotic, and the darkness had swallowed him whole. Elias, alone and vulnerable, was left to navigate this nightmarish realm.

Despair threatened to engulf him. The weight of his past, the horrors he'd witnessed, the betrayals he'd endured, all pressed down on him, threatening to crush his spirit. He was a broken man, traversing a broken world. Yet, strangely, a flicker of hope remained. A desperate, clinging ember in the suffocating darkness.

It came in the form of a sound – a low, guttural growl that resonated deep within his chest, vibrating his very bones. It wasn't the roar of the beast he'd fled, but something...different. He cautiously followed the sound, his heart hammering against his ribs, a frantic drumbeat in the oppressive silence.

He found them huddled beneath the grotesque overhang of a colossal, petrified mushroom, their forms hunched and shadowed. They were grotesque, beyond any imagining – creatures born of nightmare, their bodies a grotesque fusion of chitin and flesh, their limbs contorted and unnatural. One, larger than the others, possessed a single, colossal eye that glowed with malevolent intelligence.

Fear, raw and primal, threatened to overwhelm him. Yet, something held him back – a strange sense of...understanding. These creatures, these horrors, weren't simply mindless beasts. There was a flicker of something else in their eyes – cunning, calculation, even...regret.

The largest creature, the one with the single eye, rose slowly, its movements surprisingly fluid despite its monstrous physique. It opened its mouth, revealing rows of needle-sharp teeth, and let out a series of clicks and whistles, a language Elias didn't understand, yet somehow...felt.

He cautiously approached, his hands raised in a gesture of peace, a desperate hope flickering within him. He didn't know what he was doing, or why he was doing it, but something compelled him forward. It was a reckless gamble, a leap of faith into the abyss, but it was the only option he had.

The creatures remained motionless, observing him with their unsettling gaze. The silence stretched, thick and heavy, broken only by the occasional drip of viscous fluid from the petrified mushroom overhead. The tension was almost unbearable.

Then, slowly, hesitantly, the leader extended a clawed hand. It wasn't an attack, but an invitation. An invitation to an uneasy alliance.

Over the following days, Elias learned their language, or at least enough to communicate basic needs and ideas. He learned their names – or rather, the approximations he could make in his own tongue. He learned about their history, their suffering, their desperate struggle for survival in this nightmarish realm.

They were not simply monsters, he discovered. They were victims, just as he was. Victims of the same ancient conspiracy that had drawn him into this abyss. They were remnants of a forgotten race, warped and twisted by the malevolent energies that pulsed through this world, but possessing a shared enemy.

Their motivations were far more complex than he'd ever imagined. They harbored a deep-seated resentment towards the powerful entities that controlled the gateway, entities who had enslaved and manipulated them for centuries. Their alliance with Elias was a calculated risk, a desperate gamble to wrest control of their destiny. They needed his knowledge, his understanding of the outside world, to strike against their common foe. He, in turn, needed their strength, their intimate knowledge of the landscape, to survive.

Their alliance was born of necessity, forged in the fires of mutual desperation. It was a fragile truce, built on shared hatred and a mutual understanding of their precarious position. They were unlikely allies, an unlikely fellowship of horror and humanity, bound together by their shared plight. The monstrous alliance was a testament to the twisted nature of their reality, a reflection of the warped morals and desperate needs that defined their existence. Elias, once a man haunted by his past, was now a leader, a reluctant commander of a grotesque army, their grim purpose to survive in a world that seemed designed to destroy them.

Their initial cooperation was fraught with tension. Elias found himself constantly battling his own prejudices, his ingrained fear of these creatures, while they, in turn, struggled to trust a being from the world that had allowed the ancient entities to flourish. Their interactions were frequently punctuated by misunderstandings, almost violent outbursts, and tense silences where communication broke down completely. Yet, amidst the distrust, a grudging respect began to bloom.

Their first major challenge came in the form of a brutal encounter with a creature far larger and more powerful than any they had faced before. It was a colossal entity of writhing, obsidian flesh, its many eyes burning like malevolent stars, its maw filled with rows of razor-sharp teeth capable of rending steel. The battle was a desperate struggle, a chaotic melee of claws and teeth, of guttural roars and desperate screams.

Elias, armed with only a scavenged spear and his own wits, fought alongside his monstrous allies. He saw their strength, their ferocity, their loyalty, not to him, but to their own survival. They fought with a desperate determination he hadn't witnessed in humanity for a very long time. They were fighting not for some grand ideal, but for their right to exist, to resist, to survive in the face of annihilation. It was a fight for the very essence of their being.

They were pushed to their limits. Their allies fell one by one, sacrifices to the beast's overwhelming might. The gruesome battle left Elias wounded, battered, but alive. The loss of their comrades, especially one they had come to see as a friend, was a staggering blow to their morale, underlining the constant, ever-present threat of mortality in this broken land. The sheer survival of the fight became a sobering testament to their fortitude. They had narrowly escaped annihilation, but they knew this was far from the end. Their alliance, tested by fire and blood, was more vital now than ever.

Their victory, however, was pyrrhic. The battle left them weakened, their numbers decimated. They were forced into a strategic retreat, seeking refuge in a hidden sanctuary deep within the forbidden realm – a forgotten city shrouded in perpetual twilight, where the ancient civilization had once thrived.

This retreat forced a profound change in their uneasy alliance. Survival now depended upon a new level of trust, a shared understanding of vulnerability. The loss of their comrades, the shared near-death experience, forged a bond stronger than any they had experienced in the past. The common goal of survival replaced the previous, tentative alliances. The shared experience of violence made them realize that they needed each other more than ever.

In this sanctuary, amidst the crumbling ruins of a civilization lost to time, Elias discovered something astonishing, something that would redefine the trajectory of their struggle for survival. They uncovered evidence that spoke of a way to exploit the very entities that sought to control the forbidden worlds. Their common enemy, the ancient entity, possessed a crucial weakness. A weakness that, if exploited, could offer them a chance to finally break free from the shadows of their oppressive reign. The alliance had found their true purpose. Their shared trauma had given birth to an unexpected strength.

The weight of this discovery bore down on Elias with crushing intensity. He had come to understand these beings, not as mere monsters, but as victims, as sufferers, as fighters against overwhelming odds. Their monstrous exteriors hid their courage and their determination to break free from their confinement. He understood their plight. He understood their pain. And he understood their desperate hope for a future beyond this twisted reality. Their hope had become his own. He looked at his monstrous allies, and for the first time, he saw them as something other than a mere means to an end. He saw reflections of himself in their tortured eyes.

The discovery of this weakness had profound implications for their plans, demanding a drastic shift in strategy. They would no longer merely survive; they would fight back. They would fight for themselves, for each other, and for the slim possibility of a future beyond the nightmares that had engulfed their lives. The monstrous alliance was now more than just a pact for survival – it was a fight for freedom.

The creature emerged from the swirling vortex of shadows that had been their unwelcome guide through this nightmarish realm. It was a grotesque parody of nature, a fusion of nightmare and reality that defied rational comprehension. Towering over them, its form shifted and pulsed, an oily, obsidian carapace shifting and reforming, revealing glimpses of writhing, internal organs beneath. Tendrils, tipped with razor-sharp barbs, lashed out, tearing at the decaying trees with horrifying ease. Its eyes, twin pits of incandescent malice, fixed on Elias and his companions.

Fear, cold and visceral, tightened its icy grip on Elias's heart. Even with the grim determination forged in the crucible of their shared survival, a primal terror threatened to overwhelm him. His allies, hardened veterans of this hellish landscape, reacted with grim efficiency. Kael, the grizzled warrior whose scarred face mirrored a life of brutal combat, raised his obsidian axe, the polished surface reflecting the creature's monstrous form. His movements were fluid, a dance of practiced death honed over countless battles against horrors beyond human imagining. Beside him, Lyra, the enigmatic sorceress whose power was as unpredictable as the storm clouds that roamed this forsaken land, chanted in a guttural tongue, her hands weaving intricate patterns in the air. The air crackled with arcane energy, a tangible force that seemed to shimmer and writhe like a living thing.

The creature roared, a sound that seemed to tear at the fabric of reality itself, and launched itself at Kael. The warrior met its charge head-on, his axe biting deep into the creature's carapace, sending sparks of infernal energy flying. The impact sent Kael reeling, but he recovered with surprising speed, his movements a blur of controlled fury as he fought to free his axe from the creature's tenacious grip.

Lyra's incantations reached a fever pitch, and a wave of searing energy slammed into the creature, forcing it back. It shrieked, a sound like grinding stone and shattered glass, its form convulsing as it absorbed the full force of her attack. But the creature was resilient, its monstrous vitality seemingly limitless. The wounds inflicted by Kael's axe, deep and grievous as they were, began to close at an alarming rate. Its form flickered and reformed, the wounds sealing themselves like a grotesque, living scar.

Elias, armed with a crudely fashioned spear crafted from the bone of some long-dead monstrosity, watched the brutal exchange with a mixture of fear and grim fascination. His initial terror was slowly being replaced by a grim, cold resolve. He knew that if he failed to act, his companions would not survive this encounter. He had seen the strength, the relentless brutality, the sheer resilience of these creatures firsthand. He lunged forward, aiming for a chink in the creature's armour, a weakness they had discovered only hours earlier—a pulsating nodule on its underbelly, seemingly the source of its grotesque vitality.

His spear struck true, piercing the creature's hardened hide and finding its mark. A shriek of agony, even more piercing than before, tore through the air, and the creature recoiled, its movements slowing momentarily. Lyra seized the opportunity, her incantations weaving a tapestry of arcane energy that intensified the effects of Elias's attack. The creature's movements became sluggish, its attacks less precise. But even in its weakened state, it remained a formidable opponent. Its barbs tore at Kael's armour, drawing blood, and its sheer bulk threatened to overwhelm them.

The battle raged for what felt like an eternity, a macabre dance of death and survival played out against the backdrop of this nightmarish landscape. Elias, fighting with a ferocity that surprised even himself, continued to target the pulsating nodule. Each thrust of his spear drained a sliver of the creature's vitality, weakening its monstrous resilience. Kael, his body battered and bleeding, fought with the grim determination of a man who knew his life hung in the balance. Lyra, her face streaked with sweat, continued her assault, her incantations a storm of arcane power.

As the creature's vitality ebbed, its form began to unravel. Its carapace cracked and crumbled, revealing a pulsing mass of writhing flesh and bone beneath. Its roars became weaker, its attacks less frequent. Finally, with a final, despairing shriek, it collapsed, its monstrous form dissolving into a pool of black ichor that seeped into the earth, leaving behind only a lingering stench of decay and the chilling silence of this nightmarish world.

Exhausted but victorious, the three of them stood amidst the aftermath of their brutal encounter, their bodies battered and their spirits bruised. They had survived, but the cost had been high. Kael's wounds were deep, and Lyra's arcane energies had left her drained, her body trembling with exhaustion. Elias, despite his own injuries, felt a strange sense of exhilaration. He had faced a creature born of nightmares, and he had prevailed. But the victory was bittersweet, a stark reminder of the horrors that lurked within this forbidden realm. The silence that followed was profound, broken only by the rustling of the twisted trees and the chilling whisper of the wind. The air, though still thick with the stench of decay, seemed slightly less oppressive. For the moment, at least, they were safe. But they knew, with a chilling certainty, that this was only a temporary reprieve. The dangers of this world were endless, and their journey was far from over. The shadows held countless other threats, waiting for their next misstep.

Their immediate priority was tending to their wounds and assessing the situation. Kael, despite his injuries, possessed a pragmatic resilience, immediately beginning to assess their supplies and plan their next course of action. Lyra, despite her exhaustion, muttered incantations under her breath, drawing upon her remaining reserves of magical energy to bolster their defenses and heal their wounds as best she could. Elias, his hands trembling slightly, cleaned and bandaged his own injuries, his mind racing with the implications of their victory. They had struck a blow against the forces that controlled this nightmarish world, a significant victory, but it was a small victory in the face of overwhelming odds.

As they prepared themselves for the next inevitable encounter, a chilling realization washed over Elias. This wasn't just a struggle for survival, but a battle against an ancient malevolence, an entity whose reach extended far beyond this forsaken landscape. The creature they had slain was but one pawn in a larger, more sinister game. The monstrous alliance they had forged, born from necessity and desperation, was now more crucial than ever before. Their survival, and perhaps even the fate of humanity, depended on their continued collaboration, their shared commitment to fight against the encroaching darkness. The nightmarish realm that enveloped them held secrets that could destroy them all. And as they looked at one another, their shared determination shone through the shadows, a beacon of hope in the face of encroaching despair. Their journey had just begun, and it would be filled with unimaginable terrors.

Their rest was short, a necessary respite before the next challenge. They knew the victory over this single creature was a fleeting moment in the larger war they were fighting. The whispers of other, far greater terrors echoed in their ears, promising even more brutal encounters in the days to come. The knowledge of their limitations served as both a spur and a sobering reminder of the precariousness of their position. They were not merely battling monsters; they were battling the very fabric of this broken world, a reality warped by ancient evils and fuelled by a malevolence that extended beyond their wildest nightmares.

The chilling silence of the aftermath underscored the gravity of their situation. They had achieved a hard-won victory, a significant milestone, but the path ahead remained fraught with dangers. This monstrous alliance wasn't merely a pact for survival—it was a desperate gamble, a wager against unimaginable odds. The fate of humanity itself might hang in the balance of their success or failure. The whispers of the encroaching darkness were a constant reminder of the overwhelming task ahead.

Their bond, strengthened in the crucible of the battle, provided a fragile source of comfort, a lifeline in the face of overwhelming fear. They knew that they could not afford to falter, to succumb to the despair that threatened to consume them. Their shared journey had become a testament to their resilience, a constant push towards a goal that seemed to retreat with every step they took.

The fight, they knew, was far from over. The nightmarish realm awaited their next encounter, promising new terrors and fresh challenges, pushing their resolve to its limits. The monstrous alliance would be tested again and again, and their survival hinged on their unwavering commitment to one another, a commitment forged in blood and sacrifice. The road ahead was long and arduous, filled with unimaginable horrors, but they would face them together. They would persevere. Or perish trying.

The creature's roar, a sound that scraped against the very soul, echoed through the twisted, skeletal trees. Its attack had been swift, brutal, a maelstrom of razor-sharp barbs and suffocating shadow. They'd barely escaped with their lives, Isadora's arcane shield flickering and failing, leaving them exposed to the creature's sickening gaze. Even now, the image of its writhing, internal organs, glimpsed beneath its shifting carapace, burned itself onto Elias's mind.

Anya, her face pale and drawn, stumbled, her breath ragged. A deep gash, bleeding profusely, marred her arm, a testament to the creature's ferocity. Elias, his own body aching from the exertion and near-death experience, knelt beside her, his hands trembling as he applied a crude bandage fashioned from torn strips of his already tattered cloak. The air hung heavy with the stench of decay and something else, something ancient and malevolent, a pervasive odor that seemed to seep into their very bones.

"We need to go," Isadora rasped, her voice strained, her eyes scanning their surroundings with a desperate urgency. The shadows writhed and pulsed around them, promising more terrors to come. The air itself felt charged with malice, a palpable sense of dread pressing down on them. Their initial sense of cautious optimism, born from their unlikely alliance and initial successes, had been brutally shattered. The monstrous realm was not as passive as they initially hoped.

Elias nodded, his gaze falling upon the broken, moss-covered stones that formed a rough, barely visible pathway. It twisted and turned into the heart of the forbidding forest, beckoning them further into the oppressive darkness. Their previous plan was now a mangled relic of a naive past. They had hoped to navigate the treacherous landscape and find a way to seal the gateway. Now, survival was the only goal.

Their retreat was a desperate scramble, a frantic flight through a landscape that seemed determined to swallow them whole. Twisted trees clawed at them, their gnarled branches snagging at their clothes. The ground beneath their feet was treacherous, a shifting mire of decaying vegetation and hidden pitfalls. They moved in near-silence, the only sound the frantic beating of their hearts and the occasional rasp of their ragged breaths.

The forest itself seemed to press in on them, a suffocating embrace of darkness and decay. The air was thick with the scent of damp earth, rotting wood, and something else, something indescribably foul, a smell that hinted at unspeakable horrors lurking just beyond the edge of their vision. Every shadow seemed to writhe and shift, playing tricks on their eyes, conjuring visions of grotesque creatures lurking just beyond their reach. Paranoia, fueled by exhaustion and fear, gnawed at their resolve. They were hunted, not just by the monstrous being they had encountered, but by the very essence of the realm itself.

They pressed onward, driven by a primal instinct for survival. Anya, despite her injury, maintained a surprising resilience, her determination fueled by an unwavering sense of purpose. Isadora, her arcane power waning, relied on her sharp intellect and keen observation skills, guiding them through the treacherous maze of the forest. And Elias, haunted by his past and consumed by the weight of his present predicament, found a strength he didn't know he possessed, a grim determination to see this through. Their reliance on each other transformed from a strategy to a desperate need; one faltering would drag the others down.

After what felt like an eternity, they stumbled upon a narrow cleft in the earth, hidden amongst the roots of an ancient, decaying tree. It was barely visible, almost swallowed by the encroaching darkness. It was a narrow passage, barely wide enough for a person to squeeze through, leading downwards into the earth. It smelled of damp earth and something else, something strangely sweet and unsettling. A faint, ethereal glow emanated from within. Hope, a flickering candle in the overwhelming darkness, ignited within them.

They hesitated only for a moment. The alternative – to remain in the open, exposed to the horrors of this nightmarish realm – was unthinkable. They squeezed through the narrow opening one by one, their bodies bruised and battered, their spirits broken but not defeated.

The passage led them down a steep incline, into a subterranean chamber. The air within was surprisingly warm and humid, a stark contrast to the cold, damp air of the forest above. The ethereal glow intensified, revealing a vast, cavernous space, illuminated by phosphorescent fungi that clung to the walls and ceiling. The chamber was oddly beautiful, in a grotesque, unsettling way. Stalactites, formed from some unknown, alien mineral, hung from the ceiling like grotesque teeth, their surfaces shimmering with an unnatural light.

At the far end of the chamber, nestled amongst the strange, glowing fungi, was a pool of water, its surface as still as glass, reflecting the ethereal light back up into the cavernous space. The water itself shimmered with an otherworldly luminescence, and around its edge, strange, plant-like formations, resembling luminous coral, pulsed with a gentle, rhythmic glow.

As they approached the pool, they heard a low, guttural sound, a soft murmur that seemed to resonate deep within the very heart of the cavern. It was a voice, but not a voice in the conventional sense. It was more of a feeling, a vibration, a sensation that seeped into their minds, filling them with both dread and a strange, almost seductive curiosity. They couldn't understand the words, but they understood the intent: warning. An ancient power resided here, a power both benevolent and malevolent. They were not welcome. They were being observed.

Suddenly, a figure emerged from the shadows at the far end of the chamber. It was humanoid in form, but its features were impossibly distorted, its skin a patchwork of unnatural colors and textures. Its eyes glowed with an eerie intelligence, radiating malice and an unnerving curiosity. This was no creature of flesh and blood, but something older, something beyond human comprehension. It raised a hand, a gesture both threatening and strangely graceful, and spoke in a voice that was both ancient and oddly soothing. A language alien yet somehow familiar, a melody that evoked forgotten memories and primal fears.

The creature, they realised, was a protector of this hidden sanctuary – and a terrifying gatekeeper. Their strategic retreat had led them to a haven, yes, but it came at the price of a terrifying encounter with an unknown entity that now held their fate in its grotesque, luminous hands. Their journey was far from over. The monstrous alliance, fragile as it was, had a new challenge to face. The test was no longer just their own survival against the horrors of the Forbidden Worlds, but to determine if they could survive this new, sinister encounter.

The air hung heavy with the scent of decay and damp earth, a miasma clinging to the gnarled roots of the ancient trees that formed their precarious sanctuary. Silence, thick and oppressive, had settled after the creature's retreat, a silence more terrifying than the beast's roar. Isadora, her face pale and drawn, leaned against the rough bark of a tree, her breath coming in ragged gasps. The arcane shield, shimmering faintly now, pulsed with a weak, erratic light, a testament to the strain it had endured. Elias, his hands trembling, examined his own wounds; deep gashes that pulsed with a dull, throbbing pain. He could taste blood, metallic and acrid on his tongue.

He looked at Isadora, her normally vibrant eyes clouded with a weariness that went beyond physical exhaustion. There was a flicker of something else in their depths – a grim determination, a shadow of resignation. He knew, instinctively, that something was wrong. Something had shifted between them, a subtle change in the dynamic that had held their fragile alliance together.

"The creature... it was guarding something," Isadora finally rasped, her voice barely a whisper, each word a painful effort. She gestured with a trembling hand towards a cavern hidden deep within the gnarled roots of the ancient trees, its entrance obscured by a curtain of moss and shadows. "A gateway. A way out... or perhaps, a way deeper in."

Elias felt a cold dread crawl up his spine. He had anticipated challenges, the constant threat of the monstrous denizens of this nightmarish realm, but this... this felt different. This felt like a choice, a sacrifice looming on the horizon. He moved towards the cavern, his hand instinctively reaching for the hilt of his worn dagger, its edge dulled but still deadly. He didn't need to ask what Isadora was implying. He already knew.

The cavern was choked with the same oppressive silence as the forest outside, only amplified by the claustrophobic darkness. The air grew colder, the scent of decay intensifying, a blend of rotting vegetation and something else... something ancient and unsettlingly familiar. As their eyes adjusted to the gloom, they saw it – a swirling vortex of iridescent energy, pulsating with a malevolent light. It shimmered and pulsed, a gateway to... somewhere.

"It's unstable," Isadora whispered, her voice barely audible above the low hum emanating from the vortex. "The creature... it was trying to prevent its collapse. To buy us time."

Elias felt a knot of dread tighten in his stomach. The implication hung heavy in the air, unspoken but understood. The creature, a being of immense power and terrifying savagery, had sacrificed itself to protect them, to give them a chance. The weight of that sacrifice pressed down on him, heavy and suffocating. He felt the sting of guilt, a sharp, burning sensation, like a shard of glass embedded in his heart.

"But at what cost?" Elias murmured, his voice barely above a breath. He ran his hand over the crudely carved runes on his dagger, the cool metal a small comfort against the overwhelming sense of loss. He remembered the creature's eyes, glowing with an intelligence that transcended the grotesque shell it inhabited. It was a protector, yes, but it was also a creature of unimaginable power, a force of nature warped and twisted by the malevolence of this world.

Isadora nodded slowly, her gaze fixed on the unstable gateway. "The gateway is linked to the source of this... corruption. To close it, we need to seal the source. But the source... it's within the gateway itself." She paused, her breath hitching. "The only way to seal it is to... to sacrifice something of immense power. Something that can contain the energy, absorb it." Her voice trembled slightly, barely audible. The words hung in the air like a death sentence.

Elias understood. The gateway was like a wound, a festering sore in the fabric of reality. To heal it, they needed to cauterize it, to seal it with something powerful enough to contain the monstrous energy within. And that something... that something had to be one of them. They couldn't risk the gateway collapsing. The consequences of unleashing that energy would be unimaginable. It would unleash an unrestrained flood of the monstrous horrors of the Forbidden Worlds into their own.

A long, agonizing silence filled the cavern. The only sound was the low hum of the vortex and the frantic beat of their hearts. Elias looked at Isadora, her face illuminated by the eerie glow of the gateway. He saw the same understanding reflected in her eyes, the same chilling realization. This was not a battlefield they could win. There was no glorious victory. This was about survival. A brutal, agonizing survival, bought with the blood of one of them.

"There's no other way," Isadora whispered, her voice barely a breath. Her gaze fell to her hands, and Elias saw the way her fingers, usually so graceful and deft in manipulating her arcane energies, trembled slightly. He saw the resignation in her eyes, a profound acceptance of the inevitable.

Elias knew that if they didn't close the gateway now, the monstrous creatures from the Forbidden Worlds would spill into their world, causing an unimaginable apocalypse. This place was no longer just a hidden sanctuary, it was the frontline, the last stand against an invasion from hell.

A chilling realization dawned on Elias. He knew he was going to die.

"No," Elias said, his voice firm despite the turmoil within. "It has to be me."

Isadora's eyes widened, a flicker of protest in their depths. "Elias, no! I... I'm stronger. My magic..."

He placed a hand over hers, her fingers cold and clammy. "Your magic is needed to guide me, to ensure it works. To protect what's left." He forced a smile, a weak, pained expression. "I've faced death before, Isadora. I've seen the darkest corners of my own soul. My life, compared to the lives of the countless innocents who will die if this gateway remains open, is meaningless."

Tears welled up in Isadora's eyes, and for a moment, Elias saw her struggle. This was not a noble sacrifice, this was a desperate attempt to prevent a greater horror. The decision was brutal, but necessary.

He pulled a small, intricately carved amulet from around his neck – a relic from his past, a piece of his forgotten history, imbued with a fragment of power he had never understood, a remnant of a forgotten power he never dared to utilize. He held it out to Isadora, his hands shaking.

"Use this," he rasped. "Channel your magic through it. It'll amplify your power, give you the strength to guide the energy. And ensure I don't suffer." He looked into her eyes, his own filled with the fear and determination. His voice was filled with a chilling mixture of resignation and resolve. "Remember the fallen creatures. Remember our journey. Don't let this be for nothing."

Isadora nodded, her tears flowing freely now. She took the amulet from his hand, her fingers trembling. The weight of the impending sacrifice was heavy upon them both. The decision was made. The price was set. And the sacrifice was about to begin. The cavern pulsed with the dark energy of the vortex, a menacing heartbeat echoing in the silence. Elias braced himself, ready to face the darkness, ready to pay the ultimate price for the survival of humanity.

The obsidian amulet, cool against Isadora's skin, pulsed with a faint, rhythmic thrum. The air itself vibrated, a low hum that resonated deep within Elias's bones. He watched, his heart a frantic drum against his ribs, as Isadora began the ritual, her voice a low chant in an ancient tongue, words that seemed to claw at the very fabric of reality. The cavern, previously a suffocating pressure cooker of dread, now felt strangely... fluid. The darkness itself seemed to writhe and shift, responding to the incantation.

Then, a tremor. Not the earth shaking, but a tremor in the very essence of the place, a ripple in the dark energy that pulsed from the vortex. The shimmering shield surrounding them flickered violently, its protective glow almost extinguished. Elias braced for the worst, expecting a catastrophic assault, but instead, something unexpected happened. A voice, thin and reedy, echoed from the depths of the vortex – a voice that was somehow both ancient and chillingly contemporary.

"The... the ritual... it weakens us," the voice hissed, a sound like nails scraping across a chalkboard. It was laced with a palpable agony, a torment that seemed to seep into the very air they breathed. The tremor intensified. The vortex, previously a swirling maelstrom of impenetrable darkness, began to distort, its edges fraying like a tattered shroud.

Isadora, sweat beading on her brow, didn't break her concentration. Her chanting quickened, the words gaining a feverish intensity. Elias, initially stunned by the revelation, now understood. The ritual wasn't merely a sacrifice; it was a probe, a surgical strike aimed at the heart of the monstrous alliance. The entities weren't invincible. They had a weakness. And Isadora, with her ancient knowledge and unwavering resolve, was exploiting it.

The voice from the vortex continued its desperate whispers, its agony escalating with each passing moment. Fragments of information, disjointed and terrifying, pierced the cacophony of the ritual. Elias gleaned snatches of conversations between the entities, their internal conflicts and disagreements laid bare in their moments of weakness. He learned of their dependence on a source of power he didn't yet comprehend, a malevolent energy that was being drained by Isadora's ritual. He heard their fear – a chilling, unfamiliar sound from beings who had previously seemed untouchable.

The vortex continued to deform, its swirling darkness now punctuated by rents of pure, blinding light. The air crackled with an unbearable energy, a volatile mix of primal chaos and nascent hope. Elias felt a surge of strength, a renewed determination to fight. They weren't merely surviving; they were striking a blow against the heart of darkness itself.

As Isadora's chant reached its crescendo, the vortex imploded inward, collapsing upon itself in a spectacular display of unearthly energy. A blinding flash momentarily obliterated their vision, followed by a deafening roar that shook the very foundations of the cavern. When Elias could

see again, the vortex was gone. The oppressive
weight of the darkness had lifted, leaving
behind a strange, almost unsettling silence.
The air felt cleaner, thinner, devoid of the
suffocating miasma that had clung to them for
so long.

But the victory was far from complete.
The voice from the vortex had revealed more
than just a weakness. It had also hinted at the
scale of the entities' plans, the vastness of their
influence. The monstrous alliance, while
wounded, was far from defeated. They were
regrouping, consolidating their power in the
shadows, waiting for their opportunity to strike
again. Elias knew, with a cold certainty that
settled deep in his gut, that this was merely the
first battle in a long, brutal war.

Isadora collapsed, her body drained of
energy, her face pale and drawn. The strain of
the ritual had taken its toll. Elias rushed to her
side, his heart pounding with a mixture of relief
and foreboding. He cradled her head in his lap,
his fingers tracing the delicate lines of her face,
feeling the faint tremor of her pulse against his
fingertips.

"What have we learned?" he whispered, his voice barely audible.

Isadora coughed, a rattling sound that tore at his heart. "Their power... it's tied to the Obsidian Heart," she rasped, her voice strained. "A source of unimaginable darkness... a nexus of their power. Destroy that, and we might stand a chance."

The Obsidian Heart. The name resonated with a terrible significance. Elias felt a cold dread creep into his veins. The whispers of the vortex had hinted at its location, a place of ancient power and unspeakable horror. It was a journey into the heart of darkness itself, a quest that would test their courage, their resolve, and their very souls.

He knew the price of failure. He had seen the monstrous creatures, felt the chilling embrace of the forbidden worlds. He had tasted the bitter ash of despair, and he knew the darkness was capable of unimaginable cruelty. The survival of humanity rested on their shoulders, on their ability to face the ultimate horror, and emerge victorious.

But there was something else, a new element that had entered the equation. Hope. A fragile, flickering flame in the face of overwhelming darkness. They had discovered a weakness, a chink in the armor of their seemingly invincible foes. They had struck a blow, and they had survived. That alone was a victory, a testament to their resilience, their unwavering spirit, and their shared determination to fight for a world on the brink of annihilation.

The next few hours were a blur of feverish activity. They tended to Isadora's wounds, sharing what meager rations they had left. As the first rays of dawn pierced the gloom of the cavern, a chilling realization settled upon Elias. The victory had been hard-won, but it had come at a cost. The ritual had weakened the entities, but it had also weakened them. Isadora, their most powerful ally, was near death, her life force depleted by the sheer power of the ritual.

He felt the weight of their collective exhaustion settling upon him, the stark reality of their perilous situation. The monstrous alliance might be weakened, but their threat remained potent. The Obsidian Heart, the source of their power, was still out there, awaiting its discovery. And the journey to find it, Elias knew with a chilling premonition, would be more dangerous than anything they had faced so far.

Elias looked out at the desolate landscape surrounding their sanctuary, the gnarled trees standing like skeletal sentinels against the bleak dawn. He knew they needed to act quickly, before the entities could recover their strength. They needed to find the Obsidian Heart, and they needed to destroy it before it was too late. The weight of the world, the fate of humanity, rested upon his weary shoulders. The journey had only just begun, and the darkness was waiting.

The path ahead was fraught with peril. The knowledge of the entities' weakness was a beacon of hope, but it was a fragile hope, easily extinguished. The road to the Obsidian Heart would lead them through treacherous landscapes, past lurking horrors and unimaginable dangers. The shadows held more than just monsters; they held treachery, betrayal, and the chilling possibility of defeat.

Elias knew he couldn't rely solely on brute force. He needed strategy, cunning, and allies. He would need to draw upon every ounce of his strength, physical and mental, and he would need to forge new alliances, even with those he previously considered enemies. The journey would require sacrifice, perhaps even more sacrifices than they had already made.

The air grew colder as the sun finally broke through the canopy, casting long, skeletal shadows across their makeshift sanctuary. The silence, once comforting in its stillness, now held a chilling undercurrent of anticipation. They were not alone. The entities, though weakened, were watching, waiting, plotting their next move. The fight for humanity's survival was far from over. It was, in fact, just beginning. And Elias, haunted by his past, driven by a desperate need to protect the future, was ready to face the darkness, ready to walk into the heart of hell itself. He had a weakness to exploit, a weapon to wield, and a battle to win. The fate of worlds hung in the balance.

Chapter 5:

The Heart of Darkness

The air hung thick and cloying, a miasma of decay and something far older, far more sinister. Each rasping breath tasted of ash and the metallic tang of blood, a constant reminder of the hostile landscape that pressed in from all sides. Elias, his face streaked with grime and sweat, stumbled onward, his ragged cloak offering little protection against the biting wind that carried whispers of forgotten tongues. Beside him, Xalzar, the grotesque yet strangely sympathetic creature whose obsidian skin seemed to absorb the dim light, shuffled with a disconcerting silence, its multiple eyes – unsettlingly human in their expression – fixed on the path ahead. Behind them, Lyra, the last of the ancient civilization, her ethereal beauty marred by the harshness of this world, clutched a flickering lantern, its feeble flame struggling against the encroaching darkness.

Their journey had taken them through landscapes that defied description, places where the very fabric of reality seemed to unravel. Mountains of twisted bone scraped the sky, their peaks capped with clouds of a perpetually swirling, crimson dust. Rivers of viscous, black ichor snaked through valleys choked with the skeletal remains of colossal, nameless beasts. The air itself throbbed with a malevolent energy, a palpable sense of dread that clung to them like a shroud. They had encountered creatures both terrifying and strangely beautiful, beings woven from nightmare and moonlight, their movements fluid and lethal. Each encounter had been a brutal struggle for survival, each victory purchased at a steep price.

Lyra, her voice a low, haunting whisper, recounted tales of the ancient civilization, her words painting a picture of a once-flourishing society brought low by the very forces they now sought to confront. She spoke of the Obsidian Heart, the pulsating core of this forbidden realm, a source of both immense power and unspeakable horror. It was this Heart, she explained, that fueled the malevolent entities that sought to break through into the mortal world, twisting reality and corrupting all that it touched. Reaching it, however, was proving to be a task of unimaginable difficulty.

The path twisted and turned, leading them deeper into the abyss. The ground beneath their feet shifted and groaned, the very earth seeming to writhe beneath their tread. Xalzar's senses, far keener than Elias's, guided them through the treacherous terrain, its uncanny ability to perceive hidden dangers proving invaluable. Lyra, meanwhile, deciphered cryptic symbols etched into the crumbling stone structures they encountered, piecing together fragments of the ancient civilization's history and their desperate, ultimately futile, attempts to contain the encroaching darkness. The symbols, she explained, described rituals and sacrifices, horrifying practices designed to appease the entities and prevent the catastrophic breaching of the gateway that had brought Elias into this nightmarish realm.

As they ventured deeper, the whispers intensified, growing into a cacophony of guttural moans and chilling screams. The landscape itself seemed to contort and twist around them, its features shifting and reforming in ways that strained the very boundaries of comprehension. Elias, despite the horrors he had witnessed, felt a growing sense of unease, a creeping dread that went beyond the physical dangers they faced. It was a feeling of profound wrongness, a sense of being utterly out of place in a reality that should not exist.

One particularly harrowing night, they found themselves trapped within a labyrinthine network of subterranean tunnels, the air thick with the stench of decay and the suffocating pressure of the earth above. The tunnels were infested with grotesque, subterranean creatures – pale, blind things that hunted by sound and scent, their clicks and chitters echoing through the oppressive darkness. They fought their way through hordes of these subterranean horrors, their weapons stained crimson with the creatures' viscous, phosphorescent blood. The experience left Elias shaken, the relentless assault a stark reminder of their vulnerability in this hostile world.

The further they journeyed, the more Elias began to question the very nature of this realm. Was it a physical place, or simply a manifestation of some deeper, more fundamental horror? The creatures they encountered defied all known classifications, their forms shifting and morphing, their behaviors unpredictable and unsettling. Were they products of some ancient, forbidden magic, or were they something far more primordial, far more alien? The answer, he realized, was likely far more complex and disturbing than he could comprehend.

Days bled into nights, each marked by another near-death experience, another horrific revelation. The landscape became a nightmarish kaleidoscope of impossible geometries and disturbing imagery. Elias found himself questioning his sanity, the line between reality and nightmare increasingly blurred. He started to experience vivid, nightmarish hallucinations, blurring the lines between this infernal plane and fragmented memories of his past. These visions were disturbingly consistent, hinting at a dark ritual, an event that seemed intrinsically connected to the artifact he'd found and his arrival in the forbidden world.

Finally, after what seemed like an eternity, they reached it – the Obsidian Heart. It wasn't the monolithic structure Lyra had anticipated, but rather a pulsating, organic mass of black, obsidian-like material, embedded within a cavern whose walls seemed to writhe and breathe. The Heart throbbed with a terrifying rhythm, its surface marked with intricate patterns that shifted and rearranged themselves, reflecting Lyra's described rituals. A palpable aura of malevolent energy emanated from it, a suffocating pressure that threatened to crush them.

As they approached, a chilling figure emerged from the shadows – the Guardian, a being of immense power and terrifying beauty. Its form was humanoid, yet grotesquely distorted, its skin a mosaic of shifting colors and textures. Its eyes burned with an infernal light, reflecting the malevolent energies of the Obsidian Heart. The Guardian was a formidable opponent, its power far surpassing anything Elias and his allies had faced before. The battle that followed was a harrowing test of their skills, their resolve, and their very humanity.

The fight was a chaotic ballet of death and destruction, a whirlwind of claw and tooth, of magic and raw power. Xalzar, with its brutal strength and uncanny resilience, fought with a savage ferocity, its multiple limbs a blur of motion. Lyra, drawing upon the residual magic of her civilization, unleashed devastating spells, her voice filled with the ancient power of her people. Elias, despite his growing exhaustion and mounting fear, fought with a desperate courage, drawing upon a hidden reservoir of strength he never knew he possessed.

The battle raged for hours, the cavern echoing with the clash of steel, the roar of monstrous creatures, and the screams of the dying. Just as it seemed their efforts were in vain, Lyra discovered a hidden weakness in the Guardian's defenses. Using this newly found knowledge, she channeled the energies of the Obsidian Heart, using the very power that fueled the Guardian to turn against it. It was a perilous gamble, a desperate attempt to harness the power of the darkness against itself, but Lyra's precise manipulation of the arcane energies successfully weakened the guardian. This gave Elias and Xalzar the opening they desperately needed.

The Guardian's power diminished, allowing Elias and his allies to finally overcome the seemingly insurmountable obstacle. But the victory came at a steep price. Xalzar, gravely wounded in the final confrontation, lay dying, its multiple eyes dimming, its obsidian skin losing its vibrant sheen. The cost of reaching the heart of darkness had been far greater than they had ever imagined. The journey to the Abyss had been brutal, a testament to their endurance and a sobering reminder of the horrors they had faced. Yet, they were not defeated. Their desperate journey had yielded a glimmer of hope amidst the suffocating darkness.

The path beyond the Guardian's shattered form wound deeper into a valley choked by an unnatural twilight. The air grew colder, the whispers intensifying into a cacophony of sibilant sounds that scraped against Elias's sanity. The ground, once relatively stable, became treacherous, a shifting morass of cracked earth and glistening, viscous substances that seemed to writhe beneath their feet. Lyra, her face pale and drawn, stumbled, nearly succumbing to the treacherous terrain. Elias caught her, his own exhaustion battling with a growing dread. Xalzar, his lifeblood seeping into the poisoned earth, emitted a low groan, his many eyes reflecting the sickly green glow emanating from the depths of the valley.

The ruins loomed before them like the skeletal remains of a forgotten god, vast structures of obsidian and bone-white stone clawing at the twilight sky. Jagged spires, etched with glyphs that seemed to writhe and shift before their eyes, pierced the gloom, their surfaces slick with an oily, iridescent substance that dripped and pulsed with an unsettling rhythm. The very air hummed with an ancient power, a palpable energy that both repelled and fascinated Elias. This was no mere city in ruin; this was the heart of a civilization that had touched upon powers beyond human comprehension, powers that had ultimately consumed them.

As they approached, the details of the architecture became clearer, revealing a horrifying artistry. Buildings twisted into grotesque parodies of organic forms, their surfaces adorned with bas-reliefs depicting scenes of unimaginable horror – ritual sacrifices, monstrous creatures, and figures contorted in unspeakable agony. Skulls, both human and animal, were woven into the very fabric of the structures, their empty sockets seeming to stare accusingly at the intruders. The stench intensified, a blend of decay, blood, and something else – something acrid and alien that burned in Elias's nostrils.

Lyra, her voice barely a whisper, began to translate the glyphs etched into the stone, her words tinged with a profound sadness. "They called this place...Aethelred. The City of

Whispers. It was their greatest achievement, their most terrible mistake." Her voice cracked, a single tear tracing a path through the grime on her cheek. She spoke of a civilization that had sought to unlock the secrets of the forbidden realms, a people who had dabbled in dark arts beyond human understanding. They had achieved unimaginable power, but at a terrible cost. Their obsession had driven them mad, twisting their minds and bodies into grotesque parodies of their former selves.

The city wasn't merely destroyed; it had been consumed from within, a testament to the insidious nature of the power they had sought to control. The glyphs depicted a descent into madness, a spiraling vortex of corruption that had engulfed Aethelred until nothing remained but these skeletal monuments to their hubris. Lyra spoke of a ritual, a final, desperate attempt to contain the power they had unleashed – a ritual that had ultimately failed, unleashing the horrors that now plagued this forsaken world.

They ventured deeper into the ruins, navigating through collapsed structures and treacherous pathways. The air grew heavy with the presence of something unseen, something

that watched them from the shadows. They
found chambers filled with artifacts –
intricately carved idols, grotesque masks, and
instruments of torture whose purpose Elias
could only dimly guess. Each object pulsed
with a malevolent energy, a silent testament to
the dark rituals that had once been performed
within these walls.

In one chamber, they discovered a vast
cavern, its walls adorned with murals depicting
a horrifying history. The murals showed the
city's rise to power, its descent into madness,
and finally, its horrifying end. The final panel
showed a grotesque figure, a being of
unimaginable power and corruption, emerging
from the depths of the earth, its form a
terrifying amalgamation of flesh, bone, and
shadow. This being, Lyra explained, was the
source of the city's downfall – an entity they
had inadvertently summoned, a being of pure
malevolence that had consumed Aethelred
from within.

They found a central plaza, a vast
expanse of cracked obsidian surrounded by
towering structures. In the center stood a
massive obelisk, its surface covered in intricate
carvings. The obelisk pulsed with a powerful

energy, a throbbing heart of darkness at the city's core. Lyra warned them of the danger, explaining that this was the focal point of the city's power, the source of the corruption that had spread throughout Aethelred.

As Elias approached the obelisk, he felt a surge of power, a wave of dark energy that threatened to overwhelm him. He saw visions flash before his eyes – horrifying images of ritual sacrifice, unspeakable acts of violence, and a glimpse of the entity that had consumed the city. He felt a pull, a siren song that whispered promises of power and oblivion. He fought against it, his will battling against the overwhelming force, his mind clinging to the fragile thread of sanity.

Xalzar, despite his weakening state, managed to muster his strength, his multiple eyes gleaming with a fierce determination. He emitted a low growl, a warning to the entity within the obelisk, a challenge to its power. His obsidian skin glowed with an inner light, a desperate attempt to counter the darkness radiating from the stone. Lyra chanted an ancient incantation, her voice echoing through the ruins, a desperate prayer for protection.

The obelisk shuddered, the earth trembling beneath their feet. The air crackled with energy, a tangible force that threatened to tear the world apart. The entity within the obelisk stirred, its power reaching out, seeking to consume them. Elias braced himself, knowing that this was their final stand, their ultimate confrontation with the heart of darkness. The air grew heavy with dread, the silence broken only by the low hum of the obelisk and the rasping breaths of his dying companion. The fight for survival was far from over; the true horror was only just beginning. The weight of the ancient civilization's sins pressed upon them, a suffocating burden that threatened to crush their spirits. But Elias, fuelled by a desperate hope and a burning desire to protect Lyra, stood his ground. He was no hero, but he would be damned if he would let this ancient evil destroy everything. The battle for the soul of Aethelred, and perhaps the world, was about to commence. The final confrontation loomed, a terrifying dance between light and darkness, between hope and despair, within the decaying heart of a forgotten empire.

The valley floor dipped sharply, plunging them into a chasm of suffocating darkness. The unnatural twilight above was swallowed entirely, replaced by a chilling, absolute black that pressed against Elias's eyes, a tangible void. The whispers, once a sibilant chorus, intensified into a screaming, maddening shriek that echoed within his skull. He could feel the malevolent energy coiling around him, a viscous, sentient darkness that sought to consume him, to unravel his very being.

Lyra, clinging to his arm, whimpered, her breath ragged and shallow. The viscous substance that coated the earth pulsed faintly beneath their feet, its rhythmic undulation disturbingly organic. Each step was a perilous gamble, a slow descent into the heart of an ancient, unspeakable horror. Xalzar, his body a grotesque parody of life, lay motionless, his multitudinous eyes glazed over, reflecting nothing but the encroaching darkness. His final gasp had been a chilling sigh, a release into the oppressive void.

The air thickened, becoming a suffocating weight that pressed upon their chests. Elias felt the breath constricting in his lungs, his heart hammering a frantic rhythm against his ribs. He pushed forward, driven by an almost primal instinct, a desperate need to reach the source of this malevolence before it completely enveloped him. He was no longer fighting for his survival, but for the preservation of a fragile sliver of hope. For Lyra. For the world beyond this nightmare.

Suddenly, the whispers ceased. The absolute silence was far more terrifying than the preceding cacophony. The only sound was the rhythmic thump of Elias's own pulse, a deafening drumbeat in the oppressive quiet. He held his breath, anticipating the next manifestation of this infernal realm's malice.

Then, a low growl, deep and guttural, resonated from the darkness ahead. It was not the rasping whisper of the valley, but something far more substantial, far more ancient. The ground trembled beneath their feet, the vibrations emanating from a source of immense power. Elias raised his hand, his fingers brushing against the cold, smooth surface of the obsidian blade at his hip. He knew, with a chilling certainty, that they had reached their destination. They had found the guardian.

The form materialized slowly from the darkness, a towering silhouette against the absolute black. It was humanoid in shape, but twisted and grotesque, a horrifying parody of human anatomy. Its skin was a mosaic of charred flesh and glistening, obsidian scales, its limbs impossibly elongated and contorted. Jagged protrusions, like broken bones, protruded from its back, and its head was a grotesque mask of warped features, a nightmare sculpted from the shadows themselves. Two eyes, burning with a malevolent green fire, fixed upon them with ancient hatred.

The air crackled with arcane energy, the very fabric of reality seeming to fray around the creature. Elias felt a wave of intense nausea wash over him, a sickness born not of the flesh, but of the soul. He staggered, his legs threatening to buckle beneath him, but he held firm, his gaze locked onto the monstrous guardian.

The guardian let out another growl, a sound that seemed to tear the very silence asunder. It raised a hand, its fingers long and skeletal, tipped with claws that seemed to drip with a viscous, black ichor. From its palm, a swirling vortex of energy erupted, a malevolent force that pulsed with a malevolent life of its own. Elias knew that this was no ordinary creature; this was a being of immense power, a protector of unspeakable horrors.

Lyra cried out, a strangled gasp caught in her throat. She stumbled backward, her eyes wide with terror. Elias instinctively moved in front of her, his body shielding her from the guardian's wrath. He raised his blade, the cold steel a small comfort against the overwhelming darkness. He would not let this creature harm her, even if it meant his own destruction.

The guardian advanced, its movements surprisingly fluid for a being so grotesque. The vortex of energy swirled and pulsed, growing larger, more menacing. Elias knew that he stood little chance against such a powerful foe, but he would fight. He would fight for Lyra, for the sliver of hope that remained. He would fight until his last breath.

He lunged forward, his blade a blur of motion. The obsidian blade met the guardian's energy vortex, the clash echoing with a deafening roar. Sparks of arcane energy showered them, searing the air with unbearable heat. Elias felt an agonizing shock run through his body, a searing pain that threatened to paralyze him. He stumbled back, his grip on the blade weakening.

The guardian shrieked, a sound of pure, unadulterated rage. It lunged at Elias, its claws outstretched, seeking to tear him asunder. Elias rolled aside, narrowly avoiding the creature's grasp. He scrambled to his feet, his body screaming in protest. He was injured, wounded, but not broken. He would not be broken.

He fought with a ferocity born of desperation. He danced around the guardian's attacks, his blade a blur of motion. He used his agility and cunning to evade the creature's devastating attacks, finding small openings in the creature's movements, delivering strikes that were precise and deadly. Every strike was a gamble, a desperate attempt to overcome the overwhelming power of the guardian. He felt like he was fighting against the very fabric of this malevolent realm.

The battle raged on, a terrifying dance between light and darkness, between a desperate man and an ancient guardian. The valley echoed with the clash of steel against energy, with the screams of pain and rage.

Elias fought with a ferocity he never knew he possessed, fueled by a primal need to survive, to protect Lyra, and to finally put an end to the ceaseless horrors of this forbidden realm. The fight was a blur of motion, a terrifying ballet of pain and desperation. The air was thick with the stench of ozone and blood, the very ground beneath them seemed to shudder with the intensity of their struggle. Elias knew the cost of survival here would be high. He just hoped it wouldn't be the price of Lyra's life.

He saw an opportunity, a small opening in the guardian's defenses, a weakness in its impossibly complex movements. He channeled all his remaining energy, summoning a reservoir of strength he didn't know he had, and launched himself forward, his blade aimed directly at the heart of the creature's twisted chest. The obsidian blade pierced the flesh, sinking deep into the guardian's horrifying form.

A deafening shriek ripped through the silence, a sound of raw agony that seemed to shake the very foundations of the world. The guardian recoiled, its body convulsing violently. The green fire in its eyes dimmed, flickering like a dying ember. The vortex of energy dissipated, dissolving into nothingness.

The guardian collapsed to the ground, its massive form shuddering violently before falling silent. The silence that followed was thick, heavy, pregnant with the weight of its death. The malevolent energy that had enveloped the valley dissipated, replaced by an uneasy stillness. The oppressive darkness began to recede, revealing the true horror of the guardian's demise: the chasm opened to a deeper, far more terrifying heart of darkness. The guardian was dead, but the journey was far from over.

The chasm yawned before them, a maw of impenetrable darkness that seemed to breathe with a life of its own. The air hung thick and heavy, tasting of decay and something ancient, something indescribably foul. Gone was the oppressive weight of the guardian's malevolent energy, replaced by a chilling emptiness that spoke of ages of undisturbed horror. Before them, the pathway continued, descending further into the abyss, a descent into the very heart of this forbidden world.

Seraphina, her face pale but resolute, raised her staff, its obsidian tip glowing with an ethereal, emerald light. "This is it, Elias," she whispered, her voice barely audible above the unsettling silence. "The heart of their power." Beside her, Ronan, the grizzled warrior, hefted his warhammer, its surface etched with cryptic runes that pulsed faintly with an inner light. He looked grim, his usually jovial demeanor replaced by a grim determination. His eyes, usually twinkling with mischief, were now steely, focused on the darkness ahead.

Elias, despite the chilling dread that clawed at his insides, felt a surge of grim resolve. He gripped the artifact, the obsidian shard pulsating warmly against his skin, a counterpoint to the icy chill of the chasm. He knew that this was it – the final confrontation, the desperate battle that would determine the fate of their world, perhaps even the fate of all worlds. He had faced horrors before, witnessed things that would drive lesser men mad, but this...this felt different. This felt like the end.

As they began their descent, the darkness pressed in, a suffocating blanket that seemed to sap their strength, their will. The whispers returned, no longer a chorus, but a cacophony of voices, hissing and snarling, promising oblivion. They were not merely sounds; they were tendrils of darkness, slithering into their minds, probing for weakness, for doubt. Elias fought them back, the obsidian shard pulsing with renewed strength, its energy a shield against the mental onslaught.

Suddenly, a grotesque shape emerged from the depths, a creature of nightmare made flesh. It was a colossal monstrosity, a twisted parody of life, its limbs impossibly long and thin, its skin a patchwork of decaying flesh and pulsating veins. Its eyes burned with a malevolent green fire, and its mouth, a gaping maw filled with rows of needle-sharp teeth, dripped with a viscous, black ichor. The very air around it crackled with dark energy, a palpable aura of death and decay.

Ronan roared, charging forward with his warhammer raised high. He struck the creature with savage power, the blow echoing through the chasm, but the impact was surprisingly muted. The warhammer seemed to sink into the creature's flesh, but the creature barely flinched, its eyes fixed on Elias. Ronan staggered back, his arm trembling, his face contorted in pain. The creature's flesh seemed to absorb the impact, its grotesque form barely disrupted.

Seraphina unleashed a volley of emerald bolts from her staff, each strike searing through the air, leaving trails of burning energy in its wake. The bolts impacted the creature, causing its grotesque form to writhe and spasm, but it refused to fall. The creature retaliated, lashing out with its impossibly long limbs, each strike carrying a force that sent tremors through the ground. The creature's claws, razor sharp and stained with what looked like dried blood, tore through the air, narrowly missing Seraphina, who moved with the practiced grace of a dancer, avoiding the deadly blows.

Elias, watching from a short distance, understood. This was no ordinary creature. It was an embodiment of the darkness itself, a guardian far more powerful than the one they'd faced before. He knew that brute force alone would not be enough. They had to find a weakness, a vulnerability, in this creature's horrific form. He felt the obsidian shard in his hand pulsate with renewed intensity, a surge of power coursing through his veins.

He closed his eyes, focusing his mind, feeling the pulsing energies of the shard resonating within his being. He sought the rhythm, the pattern, the underlying weakness of the creature, and he found it – a faint, rhythmic pulse within the darkness itself, a heartbeat of the forbidden world, deep within the creature's grotesque chest.

He saw it, a small, pulsating orb of dark energy nestled within the creature's chest, the very source of its strength. Elias focused the energy of the shard, channeling its power into a focused beam of light, a concentrated ray of pure energy that pierced the darkness, striking the orb.

The effect was immediate and devastating. The creature let out a deafening roar, a sound that shook the very foundations of the chasm. Its form convulsed violently, its grotesque limbs flailing wildly as the source of its power was destroyed. Its skin began to crack and peel, revealing pulsating veins of corrupted energy, which then sputtered and died. Finally, with a final, agonizing shriek, the monstrous guardian collapsed into a pile of decaying flesh and dust, dissolving into nothingness.

Silence fell again, heavier this time, filled with a profound sense of exhaustion and relief. The oppressive darkness around them receded, revealing the way forward—a path that led deeper into the heart of darkness, but now, without the monstrous guardian to obstruct their way. The battle was won, but the war was far from over. Their journey continued, deeper into the abyss, toward a destiny they could only vaguely perceive but could not avoid. The obsidian shard felt cold now in Elias's hand, the surge of power having subsided, leaving only a lingering tremor of its potent energy. The air was still thick with the stench of decay, but there was a hint of a different scent, something like ozone, and the whisperings that had plagued their journey seemed to have subsided, leaving behind an unnerving quiet. The path ahead remained shrouded in darkness, yet it now felt different. It felt...inviting. A terrible, alluring invitation to whatever horrors lay in wait.

The obsidian shard, still cold against Elias's palm, pulsed faintly, a rhythmic beat mirroring the erratic thump of his own heart. The oppressive silence of the chasm was broken only by the drip, drip, drip of unseen water, each drop echoing in the vast emptiness like a morbid metronome counting down to some unknown doom. They moved forward, cautiously, the path winding downwards into a darkness so profound it seemed to absorb even the faintest glimmer of light. Fear, a familiar companion, clung to Elias like a shroud, but it was tempered now by a sliver of something else: hope. A desperate, fragile hope, born not from optimism, but from the grim necessity of survival.

Seraphina, her face pale but resolute, moved ahead, her hand resting on the hilt of her wickedly curved blade. Behind them, Ronan, his usual boisterous demeanor subdued, scanned their surroundings with a hawk-like intensity, his staff clutched tightly in his gnarled hand. The air itself felt different here, less suffocating, less imbued with the palpable sense of malice that had permeated the upper reaches of the chasm. The stench of decay still lingered, but it was now interwoven with a subtle undercurrent of something else – a metallic tang, almost like blood, but sharper, more... ethereal.

"The guardian's energy..." Seraphina murmured, her voice barely a whisper, her eyes fixed on the obsidian shard in Elias's hand.

"It's... resonating. It's not just repelling us anymore. It's... guiding us."

Ronan nodded, his gaze sweeping across the cavern walls. "I feel it too. A faint tremor, a subtle pull. It's as if the guardian's power, its very essence, is being... channeled."

The path led them through a labyrinth of subterranean tunnels, each turn revealing more of the chasm's terrifying grandeur. Gigantic stalactites hung like monstrous teeth from the ceiling, their surfaces slick with moisture, while the floor was a treacherous expanse of jagged rocks and crumbling earth. The walls themselves seemed to writhe, shifting subtly as if under the influence of some unseen force, the very stone groaning under an immense weight. The air grew colder, the metallic scent becoming stronger, almost overpowering.

Suddenly, they reached a vast cavern, its scale dwarfing anything they had encountered before. In the center of the cavern, a colossal structure stood, its form shrouded in shadow but unmistakable in its size and ominous presence. It was a monolithic obelisk, crafted from a dark, obsidian-like stone that pulsed with an inner light, a faint, ethereal glow that seemed to emanate from within its very core. The obelisk was carved with intricate, almost alien symbols, glyphs that seemed to shift and writhe before their eyes, as if alive.

"The heart of it," Ronan breathed, his voice hushed with awe and apprehension. "The source of the guardian's power."

Elias felt a surge of power, a cold wave that washed over him, emanating from the obelisk. The obsidian shard in his hand throbbed, its glow intensifying, mirroring the pulsing light of the obelisk. He felt a connection, a strange, unsettling resonance between the shard and the massive structure before them. It was a connection both terrifying and exhilarating, a bond forged in the very heart of darkness.

Seraphina stepped forward, her eyes fixed on the obelisk. "The guardian didn't just guard this place. It... fueled it. This is the wellspring of its power, the source of its malevolence. And it's... exhausted."

The obelisk's pulsing light, while intense, seemed weaker, flickering erratically. Its power, once overwhelming, was now

diminished, exhausted, perhaps even dying.
Ronan, his eyes narrowed in concentration,
began to chant in a low, guttural tongue, a
language Elias didn't understand but felt deep
within his bones. The sounds vibrated through
the cavern, resonating with the obelisk's faint
glow, causing it to pulse faster, its light growing
momentarily stronger.

"He's drawing on the residual energy,"
Seraphina whispered, her voice filled with a
strange mix of fear and wonder. "He's
attempting to... redirect it."

Ronan's chanting intensified, his face
contorted with effort, sweat beading on his
brow. The air crackled with energy, and Elias
felt a powerful surge of power coursing through
him, linked to the obelisk, to the shard, to
Ronan's ritual. It was a dangerous game, a
delicate dance with forces beyond their
comprehension, but it was their only hope.

The obelisk's glow intensified, then
began to shift, changing color from a deep,
oppressive black to a vibrant, almost iridescent
blue. The glyphs on its surface ceased their
writhing, solidifying into static patterns,
revealing intricate scenes of celestial bodies, of

fantastical creatures, of a civilization both ancient and alien. The air filled with a strange, ethereal melody, a song of power and creation, a lament of loss and decay.

As Ronan's chanting reached its crescendo, the obelisk erupted in a blinding flash of light, its energy surging outward in a wave of pure power. Elias shielded his eyes, feeling the force of it, a raw, untamed energy that threatened to overwhelm him. He felt a strange connection to it, a horrifying intimacy, as if this ancient power were a reflection of his own tormented soul.

When the light subsided, the cavern was bathed in a soft, blue luminescence. The obelisk, now emitting a steady, calm light, no longer pulsed with a malignant energy. The metallic scent had vanished, replaced by a clean, crisp air. Silence descended, a profound silence broken only by the gentle drip, drip, drip of water, this time sounding peaceful instead of ominous.

Ronan collapsed to his knees, exhausted but triumphant. Seraphina rushed to his side, her face etched with relief. Elias looked at the obelisk, its serene glow a stark contrast to the horrors they had witnessed. The guardian's power, once a force of pure destruction, had been tamed, harnessed, redirected. It was a glimmer of hope in the heart of darkness, a fragile light in a world consumed by shadows. But the journey was far from over. The gateway remained open, and they had only just begun to understand the true extent of the threat they faced. The obsidian shard felt lighter in his hand, the connection to the obelisk lingering, a strange sense of potential humming beneath its surface. The heart of darkness had been touched, but it hadn't been healed. The battle was won, but the war was only just beginning. The true horrors of the Forbidden Worlds were still yet to be revealed. The weight of their responsibility settled upon their shoulders, a heavy burden that threatened to crush them under its immensity. Yet, for the first time since their descent into this nightmare, a flicker of true hope ignited in the hearts of Elias, Seraphina, and Ronan – a hope born from the ashes of a seemingly insurmountable foe, a testament to their strength and resilience in the face of unimaginable terror. They had stared into the abyss, and the abyss, for this fleeting moment, had blinked back.

Chapter 6:
The Architects of Despair

The putrid stench of rot lingered in the air, cloying and suffocating. Each breath felt like wading through a thick, soupy fog of death. The oppressive atmosphere pressed down on their skin, a weighty reminder of the horrors that lurked in the shadows. As they stepped cautiously through the decaying ruins, their eyes darted around, searching for any sign of movement. The eerie silence was broken only by the occasional creak or groan of the decaying structures. Every nerve in their bodies was on edge, ready to flee at the slightest hint of danger. The characters themselves were a study in contrasts. One, a hardened warrior with a haunted look in his eyes, his scarred face betraying the toll that this cursed place had taken on him. The other, a young scholar with a fierce determination burning in her gaze, driven by a thirst for knowledge and a desire to uncover the secrets hidden within these walls. But as they delved deeper into this forsaken place, they couldn't help but feel a sense of foreboding, as if they were playing a dangerous game with forces beyond their understanding. The air itself seemed to be alive with malevolence, whispering dark secrets and tempting them deeper into the abyss. In this world of decay and dread, their voices took on a character of their own. The warrior's gruff tone betrayed his weariness, while the scholar's voice was filled with a mix of excitement and trepidation. Together, they navigated the treacherous terrain, their emotions running high as they battled against the darkness that threatened to consume them. It was a place where the senses were overwhelmed, where every step brought new horrors and every breath was a struggle. But they pressed on, driven by a determination to unravel the mysteries of this cursed place, and perhaps find a glimmer of hope in the midst of all the decay and dread. Before them sprawled the obsidian citadel, a monument to despair sculpted from the very nightmares that haunted Elias's sleep. Jagged spires clawed at a sky the color of bruised plums, while grotesque gargoyles, their stone faces contorted in silent screams, leered from every shadowed crevice. This was the heart of the forbidden realm, the nexus of corruption, and the lair of their enemies.

Beside him, Lyra, the ethereal survivor from the forgotten city of Xantus, gripped her bone-carved staff, her usually luminous eyes clouded with a grim determination. Kael, the hulking, obsidian-skinned creature whose loyalty remained a precarious gamble, shifted his weight, his massive form radiating a palpable tension. Even the spectral whispers of the wind seemed to hold their breath, anticipating the confrontation that lay ahead.

"They are... different," Kael rumbled, his voice a low growl that echoed in the desolate landscape. "Not like the others. These are... architects."

The others exchanged uneasy glances. The creatures they had encountered before, horrifying as they were, were driven by instinct, by primal hunger. These entities, the architects of despair, seemed to possess a chilling intelligence, a calculated malevolence that chilled Elias to the bone.

As they approached the citadel, the air grew colder, the very ground beneath their feet seeming to vibrate with a malevolent energy. The silence was broken only by the rhythmic drip of some unseen, viscous liquid, a constant reminder of the corruption that permeated this cursed place. They passed through a gateway formed of twisted bone and writhing shadow, entering a vast cavern that seemed to stretch into an infinite abyss.

In the center of the cavern, upon a dais of polished obsidian, sat three figures. They were humanoid in form, yet utterly alien. Their skin was a shimmering, iridescent black, their eyes burning with an unholy light that seemed to pierce through Elias's very soul. Their bodies were impossibly slender, almost skeletal, yet imbued with an unnerving power. They radiated an aura of cold authority, of absolute control.

"Elias Thorne," the central figure spoke, its voice a sibilant whisper that seemed to burrow into Elias's mind. "We have been expecting you."

The voice was devoid of emotion, utterly devoid of warmth or compassion. It was the voice of pure, unadulterated evil. Elias felt a surge of fear so profound it threatened to cripple him. But behind the terror, a flicker of defiance ignited within him. He had come too far to be deterred now.

"You are the ones responsible," Elias said, his voice surprisingly steady despite the tremor in his hands. "For the gateway, for the corruption... for everything."

The central figure smiled, a slow, chilling curve of its lips that revealed rows of needle-sharp teeth. "Everything is as it should be," it hissed. "We are merely guiding the natural order, restoring balance to a world that has long forgotten its place."

"Balance?" Lyra scoffed, her voice laced with contempt. "This is not balance. This is annihilation."

The entity chuckled, a sound like the grinding of bones. "Your primitive minds cannot comprehend the grand design. We are architects, shaping reality to our vision, a vision of perfect, eternal darkness."

The conversation devolved into a tense standoff, punctuated by the chilling laughter of the entities and the strained silence of Elias and his allies. The architects revealed their plan – a complete subjugation of the mortal realm, a transformation of the world into a mirror image of their nightmarish domain. They spoke of ancient prophecies, of forgotten gods, of a cosmic order that humanity was ill-equipped to comprehend. Their words were a symphony of twisted logic and terrifying grandeur.

Elias felt a chilling recognition. The
fragments of his past, the suppressed memories
that had haunted him for years, began to
coalesce, revealing a disturbing truth. He was
connected to these entities, bound to them by a
fate he had yet to fully understand. A bond of
darkness he had yet to break.

The ensuing battle was a chaotic ballet
of shadow and light, of desperate defiance
against overwhelming power. Lyra's staff
crackled with arcane energy, her attacks
precise and deadly, while Kael unleashed the
full fury of his monstrous strength. Elias,
armed with the cryptic artifact, found himself
wielding a power he had only begun to
comprehend – a power born of the very
darkness he was fighting against.

But the architects were formidable.
They manipulated the very fabric of reality,
twisting space and time to their advantage.
Their attacks were subtle, insidious, designed
to erode their opponents' minds as much as
their bodies. Elias felt his resolve crumble, his
fear gnawing at the edges of his sanity.

In a desperate gamble, Elias realized he
must use their own weapon against them. The
artifact, he understood, was not just a key to
the gateway, but a conduit to the very source of
the entities' power – a primordial wellspring of
darkness that lay at the heart of the forbidden
realm. By manipulating the artifact, he could
disrupt the flow of that power, severing the
connection between the architects and their
nightmarish dominion.

The plan was audacious, suicidal even.
It required a level of sacrifice that tested the
limits of his courage, his resolve, and his very
humanity. He would have to delve into the
deepest abyss of his own being, confront the
darkest aspects of his soul, and risk everything
to save the mortal world from utter
annihilation. The cost would be immense. The
outcome uncertain. But failure meant the end
of everything. And Elias Thorne, haunted by
his past and driven by a desperate hope for the
future, was prepared to gamble everything.
The fate of worlds hung in the balance.

The obsidian citadel pulsed with a
malevolent energy, a heartbeat of darkness
echoing through the desolate landscape. Elias,
his breath ragged, felt the oppressive weight of

the place pressing down on him, a tangible manifestation of despair. Beside him, Seraphina, her ethereal beauty marred by a grim determination, clutched the amulet, its surface glowing faintly with an inner light that seemed to struggle against the encroaching shadows. Behind them, Kael, the grizzled warrior, stood guard, his hand never straying far from the ancient blade at his hip.

Their descent into the citadel had been a journey through concentric circles of horror. Each level revealed a deeper layer of depravity, a descent into the very heart of the forbidden realm's corruption. They'd navigated labyrinths of twisted metal and bone, bypassed chambers where grotesque experiments writhed in perpetual agony, and witnessed scenes that would forever haunt their waking hours. The air grew heavier with each step, thick with the stench of decay, a symphony of groans and whispers echoing from unseen corners.

The final chamber was unlike anything they could have imagined. It wasn't a grand hall of power, but a vast cavern, its walls pulsating with a sickly green light that seemed to eat at the very fabric of reality. In the center, suspended in a cage of writhing shadows, was the source—a colossal, pulsating heart, black as midnight, yet radiating a nauseating luminescence. Tendrils of darkness snaked out from it, feeding the very essence of the citadel, the realm itself.

"The Abyssal Heart," Seraphina whispered, her voice barely audible above the low thrumming emanating from the monstrous organ. "The source of the corruption, the engine of this nightmare."

Elias stared at it, a cold dread seeping into his bones. It was more than just a heart; it was a nexus, a focal point for unimaginable power, a gateway to something far older and more sinister than anything he had ever encountered. He felt a pull towards it, a morbid curiosity warring with the instinctive revulsion it evoked. The air thrummed with a chaotic energy, a symphony of whispers and screams that seemed to claw at his sanity.

Kael shifted uneasily, his hand tightening on his blade. "It's...alive," he muttered, his voice strained. "It feels like it's...watching us."

And it was. Elias felt it—a gaze, ancient and malevolent, penetrating his very soul, stripping away his defenses, laying bare his deepest fears and insecurities. It was a gaze that promised oblivion, a glimpse into the abyss that threatened to consume everything.

"We need to destroy it," Seraphina declared, her voice firm despite the tremor in her hands. "But how? This...this isn't something that can be simply slain."

The question hung in the air, heavy with the weight of their predicament. The Abyssal Heart pulsed rhythmically, its obscene light bathing the chamber in an unsettling glow. The closer they got, the more intense the psychic assault became. Elias felt the weight of centuries of suffering, the agony of countless souls crushed under the heel of this monstrous entity.

He remembered the ancient texts, fragments of forgotten lore that hinted at the creation of the forbidden realm. The Abyssal Heart, they said, was not born, but crafted—a weapon of unimaginable power forged by a forgotten civilization in their hubris and despair. A weapon that had turned against its creators, consuming them and their world, leaving behind only this desolate, corrupted wasteland.

"It's not just a heart," Elias said, his voice echoing in the cavern. "It's a prison. A prison for something...worse."

His words sent a ripple of fear through the group. The implications were horrifying. If the Abyssal Heart was a prison, what unspeakable horror did it contain? And what would happen if it were destroyed? Would the entity it imprisoned be unleashed upon the world?

Seraphina studied the pulsating organ, her eyes narrowed in concentration. "The amulet," she said, her voice hushed. "It resonates with the Heart. It may hold the key."

She held up the amulet, and as she did, its glow intensified, casting eerie shadows that danced and writhed on the cavern walls. A faint hum filled the air, a counterpoint to the rhythmic pulse of the Heart. It was as though the amulet was communicating with the monstrous organ, a silent dialogue between opposing forces.

As Seraphina focused her energy on the amulet, the shadows within the chamber twisted and writhed, coalescing into grotesque shapes that seemed to reach out to them, claws extended, mouths agape in silent screams. The air crackled with energy, a volatile mix of light and darkness, hope and despair.

The struggle was intense, a battle fought not with steel and magic, but with sheer will, a contest of minds and spirits. Elias felt the pressure mounting, the darkness threatening to engulf him, to drown him in the despair that permeated this cursed place. He fought back, drawing upon his inner strength, his memories of loss and suffering fueling his resolve.

The amulet pulsed brighter, bathing the chamber in an incandescent light that pushed back against the encroaching shadows. Seraphina cried out, her face contorted in a mask of pain and concentration. Slowly, painstakingly, she began to unravel the Heart's defenses, peeling back layers of corruption, revealing the terrifying truth hidden beneath.

The truth was far more horrifying than they could have ever imagined. The Abyssal

Heart wasn't just a prison; it was a parasitic entity, feeding on the life force of the realm, twisting it into a grotesque parody of existence. And within its core, nestled amidst the pulsating darkness, was something else—something ancient and immensely powerful, a being of pure malevolence that had been imprisoned for eons.

As Seraphina continued to work, the chamber began to shake, the ground trembling beneath their feet. Cracks appeared in the cavern walls, fissures spewing forth a viscous, black ichor that hissed and bubbled as it touched the ground. The air grew thick with the stench of death, and the screams of the tormented grew louder, more insistent, a cacophony of despair that threatened to shatter their sanity.

The battle raged on, a struggle for the very soul of the realm, a war between light and darkness, hope and despair. Elias fought alongside Seraphina and Kael, his courage fueled by a desperate desire to save not just the mortal world, but his own soul from the encroaching darkness. The fate of worlds hung in the balance, a precarious equilibrium between existence and annihilation. The outcome remained uncertain, a terrifying gamble with unimaginable consequences. But they would fight. They would fight to the very end. For even in the face of overwhelming darkness, a flicker of hope remained, a fragile ember against the storm. The battle for the soul of the realm was far from over.

The obsidian citadel groaned under the assault, its dark stone weeping ichor that hissed and smoked as it touched the ground. Elias, his body a tapestry of bruises and cuts, felt the familiar throb of exhaustion war against the adrenaline still coursing through his veins. Seraphina, her face streaked with grime and blood, leaned heavily against a shattered pillar, her breathing shallow and ragged. Kael, ever stoic, sheathed his blade, the metal gleaming dully under the sickly green light emanating from the citadel's heart.

Their initial assault, a furious charge fueled by desperation and adrenaline, had been met with a tide of monstrous resistance. Creatures born from the deepest recesses of nightmare – things with too many limbs, eyes that burned with unholy fire, and mouths that gaped to reveal rows of needle-sharp teeth – had swarmed them, their numbers seemingly endless. They'd fought with a ferocity born of necessity, but the cost was steep. The ground around them was littered with the broken bodies of both friend and foe, a gruesome testament to the brutal battle.

"We can't keep this up," Seraphina rasped, her voice hoarse. "They're too many."

Kael nodded grimly, his gaze sweeping over the battlefield. "The citadel...it's feeding them. As long as it stands, they will never cease."

Elias, his mind racing, understood. They weren't just fighting monsters; they were fighting the very essence of the forbidden realm, a malignant entity that drew strength from the citadel itself. Destroying the monsters was merely addressing a symptom, not the disease. To truly win, they needed to sever the connection between the two worlds, to cut off the citadel's lifeblood. But how?

He remembered the ancient texts he'd studied, fragments of forbidden knowledge gleaned from the crumbling library he'd discovered in the outer reaches of the citadel. He'd stumbled upon a passage detailing the citadel's creation – a ritual of unimaginable horror, a sacrifice of souls on an altar of despair. And it contained a clue, a cryptic reference to a "heart of shadow," a nexus point where the dimensional rift was anchored to the mortal realm. Destroying this "heart," he speculated, might sever the connection.

The plan was audacious, bordering on suicidal. It required infiltrating the citadel's deepest recesses, navigating a labyrinth of twisting corridors and perilous chambers, all while dodging the relentless onslaught of the creatures. And even if they reached the heart of shadow, there was no guarantee they could destroy it. It could be protected by powerful wards, guarded by unspeakable horrors. But it was their only hope.

"There's a way," Elias announced, his voice surprisingly steady despite the tremor in his hands. He explained his plan, the risky strategy laid bare before his companions. Silence followed, heavy and pregnant with the weight of the impending danger.

Seraphina, her eyes filled with a mixture of fear and determination, spoke first. "It's madness, Elias. The chances of success are...slim."

"It's our only chance," Elias countered, his gaze unwavering. "We can't continue to fight this endless tide. We have to strike at the source."

Kael, his expression unreadable, nodded slowly. "I'll go with you." His loyalty, unwavering even in the face of certain death, provided a flicker of hope in the suffocating darkness.

They set off under the cover of darkness, moving with the calculated precision of hunters stalking prey. The air grew heavier, the shadows deeper, as they penetrated the citadel's heart. The passages were a claustrophobic maze, the walls slick with an oily substance that seemed to writhe beneath their touch. They navigated past chambers filled with grotesque statues, their forms twisted and mutilated, their eyes burning with a malevolent light. The silence was broken only by the occasional drip of unseen moisture and the unsettling whisper of the wind weaving through the corridors.

They encountered pockets of resistance – twisted, grotesque creatures that emerged from the darkness, their forms shifting and changing, their attacks unpredictable and brutal. They fought with a desperate fury, each blow a gamble against overwhelming odds. Elias relied on his wit as much as his strength, using the environment to his advantage, luring creatures into traps, and exploiting their weaknesses. Seraphina, despite her injuries, fought with a surprising strength, her magic weaving a shield of protection around them, buying precious moments to regroup and strategize. Kael, a whirlwind of steel, hacked and slashed, his blade a blur of deadly efficiency.

As they ventured deeper, the air grew thick with a palpable sense of dread. The very stones seemed to hum with a malevolent energy, a pulsating force that resonated with the deepest fears of their hearts. They were moving towards the source of the corruption, towards the heart of the darkness that threatened to consume both worlds.

The final chamber was a vast cavern, its ceiling lost in the oppressive darkness above. At the center, upon a raised dais of obsidian, pulsed a sphere of pure darkness, the heart of shadow. It throbbed with a sickening rhythm, radiating waves of despair and horror that sent shivers down their spines. The air crackled with energy, a potent mixture of fear and pain.

Surrounding the heart of shadow, a legion of grotesque creatures stood guard, their eyes burning with an unholy fire. They were unlike anything Elias had ever encountered – beings of pure shadow, their forms shifting and twisting, their attacks impossibly swift and deadly.

"This is it," Elias whispered, his voice barely audible above the throbbing of the heart of shadow. "This is where we make our stand."

The battle that followed was unlike any they had faced before. The creatures of shadow were relentless, their numbers seemingly limitless, their attacks precise and devastating. Seraphina's magic struggled against the overwhelming darkness, her protective spells flickering and failing. Kael fought with the fury of a cornered beast, his blade cleaving through the shadows, yet always outnumbered, always on the defensive.

Elias, however, had a different plan. He had realized that destroying the heart of shadow directly might be impossible. But perhaps, weakening it, disrupting its connection, would be enough. He'd studied the ancient texts, and he knew there was a specific ritual, a counter-spell of sorts, that could disrupt the dimensional rift. It was a dangerous gamble, requiring precise timing and the channeling of immense magical energy. Failure would mean their annihilation. Success...success was uncertain, but it was their only remaining hope.

He began the ritual, a series of intricate hand gestures and incantations, his voice strained but resolute. The air around him crackled with energy, a raw power that threatened to tear him apart. He could feel the heart of shadow's malevolent energy pushing back, attempting to crush him, to extinguish the light of his will. But Elias persevered, his determination fueled by the desperate hope that he could save his world, his soul.

As the ritual reached its climax, a blinding light erupted from Elias, a surge of pure energy that clashed with the heart of shadow's darkness. The cavern shook, the ground trembled, and the creatures of shadow shrieked in agony as the rift began to destabilize. The connection between the two worlds was weakening, the forbidden realm reeling from the blow.

Whether he had succeeded remained uncertain, whether they could ever truly be rid of the horrors he had unleashed, yet as the citadel began to crumble, and the creatures of shadow disintegrated into wisps of smoke, he knew it was worth the gamble. Their fight was far from over, yet, at that moment, Elias felt the weight on his soul lessen, a tentative hope emerging from the darkness that threatened to consume him whole.

The acrid smell of ozone and burning flesh hung heavy in the air as the obsidian citadel crumbled. The monstrous entities that had poured from its depths were gone, reduced to flickering shadows that dissolved into nothingness. But the victory felt hollow, a fleeting respite in a war that had only just begun. Seraphina coughed, a rattling sound that tore through the silence, her hand clutching a wound that bled freely despite her efforts to staunch it. Kael, his usually impassive face etched with grim determination, examined their surroundings, his eyes scanning the debris for any lingering threats.

Elias, however, felt a different kind of unease gnawing at him, a cold dread that went beyond the physical exhaustion. The citadel's collapse had revealed a hidden chamber, a grotesque mockery of a sanctuary, where a horrifying truth lay exposed. On a dais of twisted bone, bathed in an unnatural, phosphorescent glow, lay a massive tome bound in human skin. Its pages, filled with arcane symbols that seemed to writhe and shift before his eyes, spoke of a ritual, a sacrifice of unimaginable horror.

The ritual, as Elias painstakingly deciphered its cryptic language, detailed the creation of the very creatures they had just fought. It was a pact, a dark bargain struck between a forgotten sect of mages and entities from the forbidden worlds. The mages, seeking power beyond mortal comprehension, had offered a sacrifice: the lifeblood of an entire village, their souls twisted and corrupted to fuel the creation of these nightmarish beings. The tome revealed the location of the village – a place swallowed by the encroaching shadows long ago, its remnants now a festering wound upon the land.

A sickening wave of nausea washed over Elias. The very ground beneath his feet seemed to tremble with the weight of this newly revealed atrocity. He understood now. The citadel wasn't just a prison; it was a breeding ground, a monstrous nursery. And the sacrifice wasn't complete. The ritual described a final, culminating act – a sacrifice of immense power, a human heart imbued with a specific magical resonance, to unleash the full potential of these creatures and open a permanent gateway between worlds.

He looked at Seraphina, her pale face a mask of pain and exhaustion. Her hand, still clutching her wound, trembled. He had trusted her, relied on her knowledge, her seemingly unwavering loyalty. But a seed of doubt had taken root in his mind. The tome hinted at a deeper betrayal, a conspiracy that reached further than he had ever imagined. Seraphina's knowledge of the forbidden worlds, her familiarity with the creatures they had fought, were unsettlingly precise. Had she known about the sacrifice all along? Had she played a part in it?

His gaze shifted to Kael, his expression unreadable as always. The stoic warrior had remained silent, a silent observer during the decipherment of the tome. But his silence was deafening, a wall concealing an unknown truth. Elias remembered the whispers he had overheard, fragments of conversations between Kael and others – vague allusions to an ancient order, a hidden agenda, the pursuit of ultimate power. The possibility struck him like a physical blow: Could Kael too be involved in this heinous conspiracy?

The weight of his suspicions was crushing. Trust, he realized, was a dangerous luxury in this world of shadows and deceit. Every alliance, every bond forged in the fires of their shared struggle, could unravel at any moment. The lines between friend and foe were blurred, indistinct in the creeping darkness.

The next few hours were spent in agonizing deliberation. Elias, driven by a desperate need to confirm or deny his suspicions, confronted Seraphina and Kael separately. His questioning was subtle, indirect, aiming to unveil the truth without revealing his own suspicions. Seraphina, when confronted with the details from the tome, reacted with a mixture of horror and denial, insisting she knew nothing of the ritual's specifics. But her explanations lacked conviction, her eyes flickered with an unshed emotion that Elias couldn't quite decipher – fear? Guilt? Or something far more sinister?

Kael, as always, remained stoic, his answers measured and precise, yet evasive. He admitted to having knowledge of an ancient order, but denied any involvement in the sacrifice or the unfolding conspiracy. His explanations, however, were laced with ambiguities, his words chosen with calculated precision, leaving room for both confirmation and denial. Elias sensed deception, a skillful performance orchestrated by a master manipulator.

The sun dipped below the horizon, casting long, ominous shadows across the ravaged landscape. The air grew colder, the silence punctuated by the distant cries of unseen creatures. Elias knew he couldn't rely on either of his companions. He was alone, surrounded by potential enemies disguised as allies. The choices before him were agonizing. He could trust neither Seraphina nor Kael fully, yet he needed their help to prevent the final, catastrophic sacrifice. He could try to expose them, to turn them against each other, hoping to find the truth amidst the ensuing chaos. Or he could forge ahead, pretending trust while secretly plotting his next move, a dangerous gamble that could either lead to victory or utter annihilation.

The burden of his decision weighed heavily on him, a physical pressure that threatened to crush him. The lives of countless individuals rested on his shoulders, a responsibility he never asked for but couldn't afford to shirk. He had glimpsed the abyss, stared into the heart of darkness, and seen the depths of human depravity. And now, he must choose his path, knowing that every choice would come with a price, a sacrifice that might cost him everything.

He spent the night alone, wrestling with his doubts and his suspicions, replaying every interaction, searching for clues, trying to unravel the tangled web of deceit. He knew that the final sacrifice was imminent, the culmination of centuries of dark rituals and machinations. The fate of humanity hung precariously in the balance, teetering on the edge of a chasm of unimaginable horrors. He understood the gravity of the situation, the responsibility he carried on his shoulders. He was a pawn in a game played by far more powerful entities, and his every move could trigger catastrophic consequences.

The weight of his burden was almost unbearable. The silence of the night was broken only by the wind whistling through the shattered remnants of the obsidian citadel, a mournful dirge for a world teetering on the brink of collapse. Elias knew that he couldn't trust anyone completely, that betrayal was as likely as loyalty, perhaps even more so. The closer he got to the truth, the more terrifying the reality became, and the more difficult it became to distinguish between the monsters that lurked within the forbidden worlds and the monsters that walked among them in the mortal realm.

He realized that the true architects of despair weren't just the entities from the forbidden realms; they were the men and women who had willingly embraced darkness, who had traded their humanity for power, who had orchestrated centuries of suffering and sacrifice to achieve their twisted goals. The sacrifice wasn't just about a human heart; it was about the sacrifice of trust, of loyalty, of faith in humanity itself. The battle for survival was not only against the creatures from beyond the veil but against the insidious corruption that festered within, a darkness that had infected the very souls of those he once considered his allies.

As dawn approached, painting the sky with hues of blood orange and sickly green, Elias made his decision. He would play his hand cautiously, trusting no one entirely, using their own ambitions and desires against them. He would expose their betrayals, one by one, if necessary, even if it meant walking a path paved with broken alliances and shattered friendships. The fate of humanity depended on it, even if it meant sacrificing everything he held dear, including any remnants of hope. The game had begun, and the stakes were higher than he could have ever imagined. The road ahead was treacherous, fraught with danger and deceit. His journey to seal the gateway and prevent the ultimate apocalypse had just entered its most perilous phase. The battle for survival was far from over.

The obsidian shards crunched under Elias's boots, a mournful symphony accompanying the silence that had fallen upon the ravaged landscape. The air, thick with the stench of decay and ozone, felt heavy, pressing down on him like a physical weight. His victory, if it could even be called that, tasted like ash in his mouth. The citadel, once a formidable bastion of unimaginable horror, lay in ruins, a testament to the brutal battle they had just endured. But the cost... the cost was staggering.

Seraphina, her face pale and drawn, leaned against a crumbling wall, her breath coming in ragged gasps. The wound on her side, a gruesome gash inflicted by one of the obsidian entities, pulsed with a sickly crimson light. Kael, his usually stoic demeanor fractured, knelt beside her, his hands moving with practiced efficiency as he tended to her injuries. His usually sharp gaze was clouded with a weariness that spoke of battles fought and losses endured. Even the resilient Kael, seemingly impervious to the horrors of their world, showed cracks in his armor.

The air crackled with residual energy, a phantom echo of the apocalyptic struggle that had just concluded. The ground trembled subtly, a reminder that the earth itself had borne witness to unspeakable horrors. Elias felt a profound exhaustion settle over him, a weariness that reached far beyond the physical. The psychic toll of confronting such unimaginable evil was almost as debilitating as the physical wounds. He had pushed himself to the very brink, and the reverberations of that effort still pulsed through his body.

He looked around at the devastation, the shattered remnants of a battle that had left a scar upon the very fabric of reality. The success of his plan – a desperate gamble involving a carefully orchestrated manipulation of the entities' own power against them – had resulted in the temporary retreat of the creatures, but not their defeat. He had managed to destabilize their grip on this plane of existence, causing a significant disruption in their power, but their retreat was not surrender. It was a strategic withdrawal, a regrouping before the next offensive.

The obsidian entities, creatures of pure nightmare, had been driven back, yet the victory felt more like a reprieve than a decisive blow. Their essence, a malignant contagion, still lingered in the air, a silent threat that promised future conflicts. Elias knew that this was not an end, but a mere intermission in a far greater, far more terrifying war. He glanced at the sky, now bleeding into the bruised purples and grays of twilight, and a cold dread settled in his heart. The night was coming, and with it, the chilling certainty of further confrontations.

His gaze fell upon a fallen entity, its once formidable form now reduced to a grotesque parody of its former self. Even in death, the creature exuded an aura of malevolent power, its obsidian flesh still shimmering with an unnatural energy. He approached cautiously, studying the creature with a mixture of fascination and revulsion. Its form offered glimpses into the terrifying mechanisms of its power, insights he desperately needed to understand. He carefully collected a fragment of the creature's obsidian flesh, its cold surface jarring against his skin. This would be an invaluable tool for further research.

His mind raced, sifting through the events of the past few hours. He had manipulated the ancient runes etched into the citadel's walls, twisting their inherent power to create a chaotic surge of energy that had momentarily overwhelmed the entities. But the runes themselves were ancient and enigmatic, imbued with a power that he barely understood. He'd risked everything, pushing the boundaries of magic and risking a catastrophic backlash. The very act had strained his own abilities to their limit, leaving him depleted and vulnerable.

He remembered Seraphina's desperate cry, the raw pain in her voice echoing the agony of the battle. He remembered Kael's grim determination, his silent strength a bulwark against the encroaching darkness. And he remembered the terrifying realization that the entities were not merely mindless beasts. They possessed a twisted intelligence, a chilling capacity for strategic planning and adaptation. This was a war of wits, and they were far from winning.

The weight of responsibility pressed down on him. He was not just fighting for his survival; he was fighting for the survival of humanity. The gateway to the forbidden worlds remained open, a gaping wound in the fabric of reality, a constant threat looming over the mortal realm. He had won a battle, but the war was far from over.

As darkness descended, casting long, menacing shadows across the ruined citadel, Elias felt a profound sense of isolation. The silence of the night was broken only by the occasional groan of the collapsing structures and the mournful whisper of the wind. He was alone with his thoughts, his victories and his losses, the weight of his responsibility pressing down on him. He knew that the architects of despair were far from defeated; they would return, stronger and more cunning than before.

He turned his attention to the task ahead. The citadel's collapse had revealed a network of hidden tunnels and chambers, a subterranean labyrinth that extended far beneath the surface. Rumors suggested that these tunnels held ancient secrets, forgotten knowledge that might hold the key to sealing the gateway forever. But exploring these subterranean depths would be a perilous undertaking, fraught with unforeseen dangers and unimaginable terrors.

The darkness offered little comfort. The air was heavy with the oppressive weight of the impending night. The silence, punctuated only by the occasional groan of the dying citadel, was filled with an almost palpable sense of foreboding. Elias knew that the coming darkness held more than just the threat of further attacks from the obsidian entities; it held the threat of betrayal.

The whispers he'd overheard before the battle – hints of a larger conspiracy, of powerful factions vying for control over the gateway, of alliances forged and broken – haunted him now, a chilling reminder of the precariousness of his position. He couldn't trust anyone completely, not even Kael, his unwavering companion throughout this harrowing ordeal. Every interaction, every alliance, was fraught with risk.

He felt the cold steel of his blade against his palm, a comforting weight in the face of overwhelming odds. He would proceed with caution, carefully weighing every step, every decision. He would exploit the fractures within the ranks of his enemies, turning their own ambitions and desires against them. He would play the game of deception, a deadly dance of betrayal and manipulation, until he found a way to seal the gateway once and for all.

The night promised to be long and arduous, a descent into the heart of darkness itself. The ruins of the obsidian citadel became a treacherous labyrinth, a canvas painted with the chilling artistry of despair. With each step, he felt the weight of the world upon his shoulders, the fate of humanity resting precariously on his ability to outwit, outmaneuver, and ultimately overcome his monstrous enemies. The coming dawn would bring no respite, only a new chapter in this horrifying, never-ending war. He pressed onward, into the darkness, armed with his wit, his blade, and a chilling determination to survive. The pyrrhic victory was merely a prelude to a far more desperate struggle, a battle for the very soul of reality. The Architects of Despair would not rest, and neither would he.

Chapter 7:

The Broken Gateway

The atmosphere was heavy with the foul odor of decomposition and electric charge, a noxious haze enveloping the devastated terrain like a funereal cloak. Where vibrant, alien flora had once thrived, now lay a desolate wasteland, the ground scarred with fissures that pulsed with an infernal glow. Twisted, skeletal remains of the monstrous beings Elias had fought clawed at the scorched earth, their forms contorted in silent agony. The gateway, once a pulsating vortex of impossible colours, was now a jagged, fractured chasm, a gaping wound in the fabric of reality, its edges smoking and spitting sparks of corrupted energy. Elias Thorne, his body a tapestry of wounds both physical and unseen, stood at its edge, the silence amplifying the pounding of his own heart.

He looked down into the abyss, a dizzying drop into a world that was both strangely beautiful and horrifically desolate. The very air vibrated with a low, guttural hum, the dying breaths of a dying world. He had succeeded. He had shattered the gateway, severing the connection between this nightmarish realm and his own. But victory felt hollow, a bitter taste on his tongue. The cost had been immense, far beyond anything he had anticipated.

The landscape bore the brunt of the conflict, a testament to the destructive power unleashed. Jagged, obsidian spires, once the proud sentinels of a forgotten civilization, now lay shattered and broken, their surfaces etched with the scars of battle. Rivers of molten rock snaked across the landscape, cooling into grotesque, obsidian formations that resembled the twisted forms of the creatures Elias had slain. The air itself seemed heavy with a lingering energy, a palpable sense of loss and despair.

His gaze fell upon the form of Lyra, the last of the Sylvani, her body nestled amongst the rubble, a single, iridescent tear tracing a path through the grime coating her face. She had sacrificed herself to empower the final blow, her life force the catalyst that shattered the gateway. Her death was a wound that ripped through Elias, a raw, agonizing pain that refused to be soothed. He had promised her a future, a chance to rebuild her shattered world. Now, there was only silence, a void where her vibrant spirit once resided.

The weight of Lyra's sacrifice pressed down on him, heavier than any physical burden. He remembered her laughter, her fierce spirit, her unwavering belief in the possibility of redemption. He felt a surge of guilt, a crushing weight of responsibility. He had failed to protect her, despite all his efforts. He had promised her a life free from the horrors of the forbidden realm, and instead, he had delivered her to the cold embrace of death.

He touched her hand, its coldness a stark reminder of her absence. Her skin, once smooth and warm, was now cold and brittle, like fine china shattered into a thousand pieces. He closed his eyes, the memory of her laughter echoing in the desolate silence, a bittersweet symphony of loss and remembrance. He felt the sting of tears, a silent tribute to the sacrifice that had saved his world.

He rose, his movements slow and deliberate, each step a testament to the physical and emotional toll he had endured. His own body screamed in protest, a symphony of aches and pains that mirrored the devastation of the landscape around him. He traced the scars that crisscrossed his flesh, the marks of a battle waged not only against monstrous creatures but also against his own inner demons. Each scar was a testament to the trials he had overcome, a reminder of the price he had paid for survival.

The silence pressed in on him, an oppressive weight that threatened to suffocate him. It was a silence broken only by the occasional groan of the dying world, a mournful dirge for the fallen. He sought solace in the memories of the battles fought, the alliances forged, the betrayals endured. He remembered the faces of his allies – the stoic determination of Kael, the fierce loyalty of Zara, the quiet strength of Theron. They were all gone, sacrificed on the altar of victory, their lives the price of humanity's survival.

The weight of his actions settled heavily upon him. He had saved his world, but at what cost? He had destroyed a realm teeming with bizarre life, a world that, despite its horrors, possessed a strange beauty. He had acted as judge and executioner, dispensing death and destruction with ruthless efficiency. Was it justified? The question echoed in the desolate landscape, a haunting melody that refused to be silenced.

He turned his gaze towards the fractured gateway, the jagged edges shimmering faintly with residual energy. He could feel the faint pulse of the forbidden realm, a whisper in the wind, a reminder that the threat was not completely eradicated. The gateway might be broken, but it was not closed. The seeds of darkness still remained, waiting for the right moment to sprout and blossom anew.

He knew that the fight was not over. He knew that the scars of this conflict would remain, etched not only on his body, but also upon his soul. He was changed, irrevocably altered by his journey into the forbidden realm. He had glimpsed the abyss, stared into the face of ultimate darkness, and emerged, bearing the scars of his survival. He had become something else, a shadow of his former self, forged in the crucible of unimaginable horrors.

The mortal world awaited him, a world forever changed by the events in the forbidden realm. He knew that he would carry the weight of his experiences, the burden of his actions, for the rest of his days. The peace that had been achieved was fragile, precarious, and haunted by the specter of what might come next. He had saved the world, but he had also lost a part of himself in the process, a sacrifice as profound as those made by his fallen allies. The scars he bore were a constant reminder of the terrible price of salvation, a price that would forever haunt his dreams.

He looked back one last time at the broken gateway, a silent testament to the epic struggle that had transpired. He knew that the forbidden realm would never truly be gone, that the whispers of its darkness would forever echo in the corridors of his memory. He had faced his demons, both internal and external, and emerged victorious, but the battle had left him irrevocably changed. He had saved humanity, but at the cost of his own peace of mind. The shadow of the forbidden realm stretched long and dark, a chilling reminder of the horrors he had witnessed and the sacrifices that had been made to secure a fragile, uncertain future. He knew that the lingering echoes of this nightmare would accompany him forever. The fragile peace felt like a temporary reprieve, a momentary lull before the storm.

The atmosphere was heavy with the foul odor of decomposition and electric charge, a noxious haze enveloping the devastated terrain like a funereal cloak. Where vibrant, alien flora had once thrived, now lay a desolate wasteland, the ground scarred with fissures that pulsed with an infernal glow. Twisted, skeletal remains of the monstrous beings Elias had fought clawed at the scorched earth, their forms contorted in silent agony. The gateway, once a pulsating vortex of impossible colours, was now a jagged, fractured chasm, a gaping wound in the fabric of reality, its edges smoking and spitting sparks of corrupted energy. Elias Thorne, his body a tapestry of wounds both physical and unseen, stood at its edge, the silence amplifying the pounding of his own heart.

He looked down into the abyss, a dizzying drop into a world that was both strangely beautiful and horrifically desolate. The very air vibrated with a low, guttural hum, the dying breaths of a dying world. He had succeeded. He had shattered the gateway, severing the connection between this nightmarish realm and his own. But victory felt hollow, a bitter taste on his tongue. The cost had been immense, far beyond anything he had anticipated.

The landscape bore the brunt of the conflict, a testament to the destructive power unleashed. Jagged, obsidian spires, once the proud sentinels of a forgotten civilization, now lay shattered and broken, their surfaces etched with the scars of battle. Rivers of molten rock snaked across the landscape, cooling into grotesque, obsidian formations that resembled the twisted forms of the creatures Elias had slain. The air itself seemed heavy with a lingering energy, a palpable sense of loss and despair.

His gaze fell upon the form of Lyra, the last of the Sylvani, her body nestled amongst the rubble, a single, iridescent tear tracing a path through the grime coating her face. She had sacrificed herself to empower the final blow, her life force the catalyst that shattered the gateway. Her death was a wound that ripped through Elias, a raw, agonizing pain that refused to be soothed. He had promised her a future, a chance to rebuild her shattered world. Now, there was only silence, a void where her vibrant spirit once resided.

The weight of Lyra's sacrifice pressed down on him, heavier than any physical burden. He remembered her laughter, her fierce spirit, her unwavering belief in the possibility of redemption. He felt a surge of guilt, a crushing weight of responsibility. He had failed to protect her, despite all his efforts. He had promised her a life free from the horrors of the forbidden realm, and instead, he had delivered her to the cold embrace of death.

He touched her hand, its coldness a stark reminder of her absence. Her skin, once smooth and warm, was now cold and brittle, like fine china shattered into a thousand pieces. He closed his eyes, the memory of her laughter echoing in the desolate silence, a bittersweet symphony of loss and remembrance. He felt the sting of tears, a silent tribute to the sacrifice that had saved his world.

He rose, his movements slow and deliberate, each step a testament to the physical and emotional toll he had endured. His own body screamed in protest, a symphony of aches and pains that mirrored the devastation of the landscape around him. He traced the scars that crisscrossed his flesh, the marks of a battle waged not only against monstrous creatures but also against his own inner demons. Each scar was a testament to the trials he had overcome, a reminder of the price he had paid for survival.

The silence pressed in on him, an oppressive weight that threatened to suffocate him. It was a silence broken only by the occasional groan of the dying world, a mournful dirge for the fallen. He sought solace in the memories of the battles fought, the alliances forged, the betrayals endured. He remembered the faces of his allies – the stoic determination of Kael, the fierce loyalty of Zara, the quiet strength of Theron. They were all gone, sacrificed on the altar of victory, their lives the price of humanity's survival.

The weight of his actions settled heavily upon him. He had saved his world, but at what cost? He had destroyed a realm teeming with bizarre life, a world that, despite its horrors, possessed a strange beauty. He had acted as judge and executioner, dispensing death and destruction with ruthless efficiency. Was it justified? The question echoed in the desolate landscape, a haunting melody that refused to be silenced.

He turned his gaze towards the fractured gateway, the jagged edges

shimmering faintly with residual energy. He
could feel the faint pulse of the forbidden
realm, a whisper in the wind, a reminder that
the threat was not completely eradicated. The
gateway might be broken, but it was not closed.
The seeds of darkness still remained, waiting
for the right moment to sprout and blossom
anew.

He knew that the fight was not over. He
knew that the scars of this conflict would
remain, etched not only on his body, but also
upon his soul. He was changed, irrevocably
altered by his journey into the forbidden realm.
He had glimpsed the abyss, stared into the face
of ultimate darkness, and emerged, bearing the
scars of his survival. He had become something
else, a shadow of his former self, forged in the
crucible of unimaginable horrors.

The mortal world awaited him, a world
forever changed by the events in the forbidden
realm. He knew that he would carry the weight
of his experiences, the burden of his actions,
for the rest of his days. The peace that had
been achieved was fragile, precarious, and
haunted by the specter of what might come
next. He had saved the world, but he had also
lost a part of himself in the process, a sacrifice

as profound as those made by his fallen allies. The scars he bore were a constant reminder of the terrible price of salvation, a price that would forever haunt his dreams.

He looked back one last time at the broken gateway, a silent testament to the epic struggle that had transpired. He knew that the forbidden realm would never truly be gone, that the whispers of its darkness would forever echo in the corridors of his memory. He had faced his demons, both internal and external, and emerged victorious, but the battle had left him irrevocably changed. He had saved humanity, but at the cost of his own peace of mind. The shadow of the forbidden realm stretched long and dark, a chilling reminder of the horrors he had witnessed and the sacrifices that had been made to secure a fragile, uncertain future. He knew that the lingering echoes of this nightmare would accompany him forever. The fragile peace felt like a temporary reprieve, a momentary lull before the storm.

Chapter 8:
The Scars Remain

The acrid stench of sulfur clung to Elias like a second skin, a constant, nauseating reminder of the hellscape he'd escaped. His clothes, once meticulously tailored, were now ragged and stained with the ichor of impossible creatures, the remnants of a war fought in a realm beyond comprehension. He ran a hand across his scarred face, the rough texture a familiar comfort in the unsettling quiet of his borrowed room. The mirror reflected a stranger: a gaunt, hollow-eyed man etched with the marks of his journey. A jagged scar, a pale, angry line, slashed across his left cheekbone, a testament to a claw that had nearly ended him. His left arm, once strong and capable, was now a patchwork of healed wounds, the flesh a testament to the brutal reality of his fight for survival. Each scar throbbed a dull, persistent ache, a physical echo of the battles fought.

But the physical wounds were the least of it. The mental scars, the fissures in his sanity, were far more insidious. Sleep offered no respite; nightmares, vivid and visceral, dragged him back into the abyss, reliving the horrors he'd endured. He saw the twisted faces of the creatures, their eyes burning with malevolent intelligence, their forms shifting and morphing in terrifying ways that defied logic and understanding. He relived the betrayal, the gut-wrenching moment when his most trusted ally turned against him, a violation of trust that left a deeper wound than any blade could inflict. He saw the death of his friend, the sacrifice that had saved him, a guilt that gnawed at his conscience, a constant, suffocating weight.

The whispers started subtly, insidious slivers of sound that slithered into the quiet corners of his mind. At first, he dismissed them as the product of exhaustion, the lingering effects of trauma. But the whispers grew bolder, more insistent, weaving themselves into his thoughts, twisting his memories, blurring the line between reality and the nightmarish world he'd left behind. They were the voices of the entities, of the creatures, their twisted essence seeping into his consciousness, a constant reminder of their existence, of their enduring power. He found himself starting conversations, his voice trailing off, leaving half-finished sentences suspended in the heavy silence of the room. The constant chatter was an internal torment.

The burden of knowledge was another heavy stone around his neck. He carried the secrets of a lost civilization, the truth of an ancient conflict, a truth that would shatter the fragile foundations of the mortal world if revealed. He knew of the entities' plans, their capacity for destruction. He bore the weight of their existence. The weight of preventing their return. It was a weight no mortal man was meant to bear.

He tried to reintegrate into the mortal world, a world that felt foreign and distant, a stark contrast to the nightmarish realm he'd inhabited. The mundane tasks, the ordinary interactions, seemed trivial, inconsequential, mere distractions from the ever-present threat he knew loomed. He was an outsider, a ghost haunted by memories that were both terrifying and incredibly real. The others couldn't see the darkness that clung to him, the echoes of the abyss that followed him like a shadow. They couldn't understand the look in his eyes, the constant, almost imperceptible twitch in his left hand. They saw a man marked by tragedy, but they couldn't comprehend the depth of his suffering, the darkness that consumed him.

The isolation was crushing. He tried to connect with others, to share his burden, but he found he couldn't. His experiences were beyond comprehension, beyond articulation. The language he needed to describe the horrors he'd witnessed simply didn't exist. His attempts at conversation were met with pitying glances, polite nods, and awkward silences. They couldn't truly understand. And even if they could, he couldn't bear to burden them with the weight of his nightmarish reality. His life was now a solitary existence. A constant dance between the terror of his past and his bleak future.

The physical world, too, had changed. Strange anomalies, subtle shifts in reality, had begun to appear, echoes of the incursion into the mortal realm. These subtle signs of decay – a lingering sulfurous smell in the air, the unnatural stillness of certain places, fleeting glimpses of impossible shapes at the edge of his vision – were constant reminders of the fragile balance he'd managed to maintain. These were things that only he saw, felt, sensed. They were further evidence that this was not the end. The conflict was not over. It was only beginning.

The past clung to him relentlessly. He was haunted by fragmented memories, glimpses of a life before the artifact, before the gateway, before the nightmare. Fragments of a happy childhood. A loving family. A home. Now only flashes of memory that felt like fragments of a dream, indistinguishable from the nightmarish realm he'd explored. These fleeting moments only served to highlight the stark reality of his current existence and the loss he had suffered. Loss of a past, a future, and possibly the salvation of humanity itself.

His actions in the forbidden realm had changed the world, irrevocably. He had saved humanity, but at a terrible cost. He had won a battle, but the war was far from over. The scars – both physical and psychological – would remain, a constant reminder of the horrors he'd endured and the burden he would carry for the rest of his days. The weight of his experience pressed down on him, a constant, suffocating presence that overshadowed every aspect of his life. He was a man broken, yet strangely whole. His transformation was complete, though his journey was far from over. The darkness from the forbidden realm continued to seep into every aspect of his existence. His battle with the entities, however successful, had not brought true peace. He was left with a constant awareness of the unseen world, a reminder of the thin veil that separated reality from the nightmare he knew would eventually return. The chilling resonance of that reality left him in perpetual fear and despair.

The silence of the room pressed in on Elias, a suffocating blanket woven from the threads of his memories. He wasn't just physically scarred; his mind was a battlefield littered with the wreckage of his experiences. The knowledge he'd gained in the Forbidden Worlds, the horrifying truths he'd uncovered, were not easily dismissed. They were a part of him now, a malignant growth twisting his perception of reality. It wasn't the physical pain that gnawed at him most, but the relentless, gnawing awareness of the fragility of the world, the thin veil separating humanity from the unfathomable horrors that lurked just beyond.

He'd seen things that would curdle the blood of even the most hardened warrior, witnessed rituals of unimaginable cruelty, and faced creatures born from the darkest recesses of the collective unconscious. He'd fought alongside beings both monstrous and sympathetic, forged alliances born of desperate necessity, and betrayed others in the name of survival. Every action, every decision, echoed in the chambers of his heart, a discordant symphony of guilt and regret. The weight of his knowledge wasn't just a burden; it was a living entity, feeding on his sanity, twisting his thoughts into grotesque parodies of their former selves.

Sleep offered little respite. Nightmares plagued him, a relentless assault of grotesque images and chilling sounds. He'd relive the battles, the screams, the agonizing deaths, each detail etched into the fabric of his dreams with excruciating clarity. He'd wake in a cold sweat, heart pounding, the stench of sulfur still clinging to the back of his throat, a phantom reminder of the abyss he'd glimpsed. Even in the moments of supposed peace, the echoes of the Forbidden Worlds haunted him. He'd find himself staring at mundane objects – a flickering flame, a shadow cast by the sun – and see in them monstrous distortions, glimpses of the chaotic reality he desperately tried to bury.

His newfound knowledge wasn't just limited to the monstrous entities he had encountered. He had also learned of a forgotten civilization, a race that had mastered arcane arts and wielded powers beyond human comprehension. Their demise had been catastrophic, a testament to the dangers inherent in tampering with forces beyond human understanding. He understood now why they had sealed the gateway, why they had sacrificed so much to keep the forbidden realms at bay. Their warnings, echoed in the crumbling ruins of their once-great city, were a chilling testament to the consequences of unchecked ambition. The knowledge of their fate hung over him, a constant reminder of the potential for future disaster. He knew, with a certainty that chilled him to the bone, that the forces he had fought were not defeated, but merely contained. A fragile peace at best.

The weight of his responsibility was equally crushing. He knew the secrets of the gateway, the weaknesses of the entities, the delicate balance that held the forbidden worlds at bay. He carried this knowledge like a venomous serpent coiled around his heart, its fangs poised to strike at any moment. He was no longer just Elias Thorne, a man haunted by his past. He was the guardian, the reluctant protector, burdened with the fate of humanity. The thought filled him with a sense of dread, a paralyzing fear that he would fail. He was a solitary figure, armed with knowledge that could save or destroy the world.

The isolation was a torment. He couldn't share his burden with others. The knowledge was too terrifying, too alien. He had tried to speak, to explain the horrors he had witnessed, but the words failed him. He was met with looks of disbelief, pity, or worse – fear. He was a man who had seen too much, a man changed irrevocably by his journey into the abyss. He was alone in his knowledge, alone in his burden, alone in his fight against the looming darkness.

Days blurred into nights, each one a monotonous cycle of fear, exhaustion, and the ever-present weight of his knowledge. He sought solace in the anonymity of the city, blending into the crowds, hoping to escape the crushing weight of his experiences. But the city itself seemed to mirror the chaos of the forbidden realms. In the shadows, in the echoes of the night, he saw glimpses of the monstrous, the uncanny, the unreal. His perception of reality was fractured, shattered by the horrors he'd witnessed. He feared that he was losing his grip on sanity, that the darkness from the forbidden realms was seeping into his soul, corrupting his very essence.

He sought solace in the books, poring over ancient texts, searching for answers, for clues to understanding the forces he had encountered. He delved into forgotten languages, arcane symbols, and the dusty pages of forgotten lore. He sought to unravel the mysteries of the forbidden realms, hoping to find a way to prevent their return. But the more he learned, the more he realized the terrifying scope of his task. The knowledge he gained only served to amplify his fear, to deepen his understanding of the unimaginable power and malice that threatened humanity.

Even in his darkest moments, a spark of hope flickered within him. It was a frail flame, easily extinguished, but it was there nonetheless. It was fueled by his memory of the sympathetic creatures he had encountered in the forbidden realms, the ones who had fought alongside him, sharing his burden, offering their support in the face of unimaginable horror. Their sacrifice, their loyalty, reminded him that he was not alone, that there was still good to be found even in the darkest corners of existence. It was a fragile hope, a slender thread in the tapestry of despair, but it was enough to keep him going, to keep him fighting against the encroaching darkness.

The physical scars were a constant reminder of his ordeal, but the psychological wounds were far more profound. He was a man forever changed, forever marked by his journey into the forbidden worlds. Yet, amidst the darkness, amidst the despair, amidst the crushing weight of his knowledge and his responsibility, he clung to the hope that he could find a way to safeguard humanity, to protect the world from the nightmare he had barely escaped. His fight was far from over. The burden he carried was immense, but so was the potential reward – the survival of humanity itself. The scars remained, a testament to his ordeal, but they were also a reminder of his strength, his resilience, his unwavering determination to fight for a world teetering on the brink of destruction. The darkness may have touched him, but it had not broken him. The battle was far from over, the war raged on. He stood on the precipice of despair, yet his gaze remained fixed on the horizon, his heart beating to the rhythm of an uncertain future.

The city lights blurred through the rain-streaked window of his apartment, a chaotic dance of color that mirrored the turmoil within Elias. He sat hunched over a half-empty bottle of whiskey, the amber liquid reflecting the flickering gaslight in a macabre imitation of his own tormented eyes. The world outside, bustling with life, felt impossibly distant, a muted symphony playing to a deaf audience. He was adrift, a ghost haunting the fringes of his own existence.

Returning had been more difficult than he'd anticipated. The crisp, clean air of the city, once a comfort, now felt suffocating, a stark contrast to the fetid, otherworldly stench of the Forbidden Worlds. The sounds – the laughter, the chatter, the mundane hum of daily life – grated on his nerves, a relentless assault on his senses, now hyper-sensitive to every nuance, every subtle shift in the atmosphere.

He'd tried to resume his life as though nothing had happened. He'd gone back to his job at the university library, a place of quiet contemplation and dusty tomes, a place that had once offered solace. But now, the towering shelves seemed to press down on him, the quiet whispers of turning pages replaced by the echoing whispers of his own fractured mind. The hushed reverence of the library patrons felt like a judgment, their quiet observations scrutinizing his every move, their normalcy a painful reminder of his profound and irreparable difference.

His colleagues, once familiar faces, now seemed distant and strange. Their casual conversations, their office banter, felt alien, meaningless. He couldn't relate to their concerns, their petty grievances, their mundane triumphs. He'd seen horrors that dwarfed anything they could ever experience, and their lives, so ordinary, felt trivial, almost mocking in their simplicity. He tried to engage, to participate, to feign normalcy, but the words caught in his throat, his attempts at conversation clumsy and stilted. A gulf had opened between him and the world, a chasm of experience too vast to bridge.

Sleep offered no escape. His nights were haunted by vivid, nightmarish visions, replays of his journey into the forbidden realm. The grotesque creatures, the malevolent entities, the sheer, overwhelming terror of it all, replayed in his mind with a sickening clarity.

He'd wake in a cold sweat, his heart pounding a
frantic rhythm against his ribs, the weight of
his memories crushing him beneath their
weight. The physical scars on his body, still
healing, ached with a dull, persistent throb, a
constant reminder of the horrors he'd endured.

Even the familiar comfort of his own
apartment felt alien. The walls seemed to close
in, the shadows to deepen, the silence to
scream. The silence was the worst. The
absence of sound, in its way, was a cacophony
of its own, a symphony of his own haunted
thoughts. He found himself avoiding mirrors,
afraid of the hollow eyes staring back at him,
the reflection of a man who no longer
recognized himself. The man in the mirror was
a stranger, a shell of his former self, bearing the
scars – both physical and psychological – of a
journey into the heart of darkness.

His relationship with Isabelle, his once
vibrant and comforting connection, was
shattered. He couldn't explain what he'd seen,
what he'd done. The words to describe the
abyss he'd stared into, the unimaginable
horrors he'd faced, simply didn't exist. He
tried, falteringly, to share snippets, fragments
of his experiences, but his descriptions

sounded like the ravings of a madman. Isabelle, initially sympathetic, became increasingly withdrawn, her concern morphing into fear and ultimately, into a heartbreaking distance. The love that had once bound them together seemed to wither under the weight of his unspoken trauma, leaving behind only a bleak wasteland of unspoken words and unanswered questions.

He tried therapy. The sterile office, the polite neutrality of the therapist, only amplified his isolation. How could he possibly explain the realities of the Forbidden Worlds to someone who had never seen them? How could he convey the terror, the despair, the sheer inhumanity of it all? His attempts at articulating his experiences were met with a well-meaning but ultimately unhelpful mixture of skepticism and pity. His therapist, a kind woman but a woman of the mundane world, could offer no solace, no understanding.

His alienation wasn't confined to his relationships. He felt it in the city itself, in the way that he moved through the bustling streets like a ghost, invisible and unheard. The laughter, the chatter, the everyday concerns of others felt distant and unreal, belonging to a world that he no longer inhabited. It was as if a veil had fallen between him and humanity, a gap that was slowly widening, leaving him isolated and alone in his private hell.

He started to withdraw further, seeking refuge in the shadows, in the quiet corners of the city that mirrored his own internal desolation. The nights were his only solace, the cloak of darkness hiding him from the judging eyes of the world. He'd wander the deserted streets, lost in his own thoughts, seeking a connection to something, anything, other than the crushing weight of his memories.

One night, wandering aimlessly through a graveyard, he came across an old, weathered tombstone. The inscription was barely legible, faded by time and weather, but he could make out a name – a name that sent a jolt of recognition through him. It was the name of someone he'd met in the Forbidden Worlds, a creature of immense power, yet surprisingly... human. The recognition was a painful stab to the heart, a reminder of the connections he'd forged in the other world, connections that were as impossible and unreachable as the world itself.

The cold stone of the tombstone felt strangely comforting, a solid anchor in a sea of uncertainty. He sat there for hours, gazing at the inscription, feeling the chill of the night seeping into his bones. In the silence of the graveyard, surrounded by the ghosts of the past, he felt a strange sense of belonging, a perverse connection to the things that were dead and gone. It wasn't a happy connection, not one born of love or belonging, but a dark, morbid comfort he found only in the shadow of death, among the things that had gone beyond his understanding and comprehension.

The rain continued to fall, washing the city in a mournful gray. Elias remained seated, the cold seeping into his bones, his mind a whirlwind of memories and regrets. The scars remained, both physical and emotional. His isolation, his alienation, was profound, a dark and lonely path with no clear end in sight. But even as despair threatened to consume him entirely, a faint flicker of defiance burned within him. The fight might be lonely, but it wasn't over. He still had the resolve, the duty to ensure the events in the Forbidden Worlds never happened again. The scars remained, a map of his journey, a testament to the nightmare he'd survived – but also a reminder

of his strength, his resilience. The fight,
however lonely, would continue. He had to
ensure that what he had seen never happened
again. The world was still at stake.

The rain had stopped, leaving behind a
city slick with a greasy sheen under the bruised
dawn. Elias, however, remained unchanged.
The whiskey bottle lay empty, a testament to a
night spent wrestling with ghosts far more
tangible than the ones he'd encountered in the
forbidden realm. He stared out at the
cityscape, a panorama of indifference to his
internal tempest. The city throbbed with a life
he felt increasingly detached from, a life that
had irrevocably shifted. The scars, both visible
and invisible, served as a constant reminder.

He ran a hand over the jagged line that
marred his left cheek, a souvenir from a
grotesque creature he barely dared to
remember. It was a physical manifestation of
the changes he'd undergone, a brand that set
him apart, a mark of the underworld's touch.
But it was the unseen scars, the ones etched
onto his soul, that truly haunted him. The
memories, vivid and agonizing, replayed
themselves in his mind like a broken record:
the screams of the dying, the stench of decay,

the cold, dead eyes of the things that lurked in the shadows.

The immediate aftermath of his ordeal had been a blur. He had stumbled back into the mortal world, a shattered vessel adrift in a sea of normalcy. The authorities, understandably, had dismissed his wild tales of otherworldly horrors as the ravings of a man driven mad by trauma. They had treated his physical wounds, but his mental scars remained, festering and unhealed. He'd sought solace in the anonymity of the city, hiding from a world that couldn't, or wouldn't, understand his experience. His apartment had become his sanctuary, a prison of self-imposed isolation.

But the world hadn't remained unchanged. He saw it in the subtle shifts, the unsettling anomalies that escaped the notice of those unaffected. The newspapers spoke of strange occurrences, unexplained disappearances, and a growing unease that permeated the city's veins. There were whispers, dark rumors that snaked through the underbelly of society, hinting at a creeping corruption, a darkness spreading from the cracks of reality. He'd dismissed them initially, attributing them to collective anxiety or mere coincidence. However, the more he observed, the more he realized that something was profoundly wrong.

He started his investigation subtly, driven by a sense of responsibility, a dark compulsion to understand and potentially mitigate the consequences of his actions in the forbidden realm. He began by revisiting the places that had been touched by the incursion—abandoned buildings, forgotten alleyways, locations that had served as gateways or battlegrounds. He found evidence, faint and subtle, but undeniably present: residual energy signatures, whispers of an unnatural presence, and an unsettling distortion in the fabric of reality itself.

One such place was an old, disused hospital on the outskirts of the city. He'd fought there, a brutal melee against beings that shouldn't have existed, yet here they were, leaving a legacy of their existence in their wake. The air hung heavy with a suffocating sense of dread, the silence broken only by the mournful creak of rusted metal and the whisper of wind whistling through shattered windows. The building itself seemed to writhe, the shadows shifting and swirling in ways that defied simple explanation. Within its decaying walls, he found strange symbols etched into the floor, a language he didn't understand but instinctively knew to be of infernal origin. The symbols pulsed with a faint, unnatural light, a malevolent heartbeat echoing the horrors he'd witnessed.

He discovered that these symbols, variations of which he'd seen in the forbidden realm, seemed to be appearing in other places throughout the city. He found them scrawled on walls, etched into gravestones, even carved into the bark of ancient trees in the city's parks. They were a silent message, a chilling testament to the slow, insidious corruption spreading through the mortal world.

His investigation led him to a network of individuals who, like him, had encountered strange phenomena or experienced inexplicable events. These were not the fringe dwellers or conspiracy theorists, but doctors, scientists, police officers—individuals with unimpeachable credentials and a shared sense of bewilderment. They had dismissed their initial observations as hallucinations, stress, or even mass hysteria. But as they compiled their experiences, a disturbing pattern began to emerge. They too had encountered residual energies, witnessed strange occurrences, and even glimpsed glimpses of the entities that he had battled in the forbidden realm.

Through them, he learned about an increase in unusual weather patterns, a surge in seemingly spontaneous illnesses, and a growing sense of unease and despair among the city's population. The changes weren't dramatic, not obvious enough to trigger widespread panic, but they were undeniable. The city felt... different. The air hung heavier, the shadows seemed deeper, and an undercurrent of fear, unspoken yet palpable, threaded through the everyday life of the city's inhabitants.

He sought the counsel of an old professor, Dr. Albright, a specialist in occult history and forgotten lore. Albright, a man consumed by his studies and haunted by his own past, recognized the symbols Elias had found. He identified them as belonging to a forgotten cult, a group that had worshipped entities from beyond the veil of reality. The cult, according to Albright, had been dormant for centuries, their influence quelled by a powerful magical seal. But the seal, weakened by Elias's actions, had started to crumble. The events in the forbidden realm, despite his efforts to seal the gateway, had caused a ripple effect, allowing this ancient evil to once again seep into the mortal world.

Albright explained that the creatures Elias had encountered were merely the vanguard, the first wave of an invasion that threatened to consume all of reality. The cult, empowered by the weakening barrier, aimed to unleash the full fury of the entities upon the world, plunging it into an age of unimaginable horror. The symbols were more than just markings; they were anchors, points of focus that allowed the entities to manifest and solidify their influence in the mortal realm.

The information sent a chill down Elias's spine. He was not just dealing with the lingering effects of his journey but the opening act of a larger, far more terrifying plan. He'd sealed the primary gateway, but he'd inadvertently opened numerous smaller cracks. He'd stopped the immediate threat, but the threat itself was far from over. His personal scars paled in comparison to the impending catastrophe. The fight, it seemed, was far from over. The battle for the mortal world had just begun, and Elias Thorne, scarred, haunted, and alone, was its unlikely champion. The weight of the world, quite literally, rested on his shoulders. The scars remained, a constant reminder of the horrors he had witnessed, and a chilling prophecy of the horrors yet to come.

The chipped porcelain mug warmed his hands, but did little to soothe the icy dread that clung to him like a shroud. He stared at the swirling tea, its amber depths mirroring the unsettling turmoil within. The encounter with the Obsidian Mirror, the gateway's temporary closure, the grotesque entities he'd faced – they were all vivid, raw wounds on his psyche, bleeding into his waking hours and staining his dreams with a horrific palette of crimson and shadow. Sleep offered no respite, only a descent into a labyrinth of nightmares where the faces of the creatures he'd fought writhed and twisted, their whispers echoing the insidious secrets he'd uncovered.

He'd always known a darkness lurked within him, a shadowy echo of a past he couldn't quite grasp. Fragments, like shattered pieces of a stained-glass window, flashed through his memory: the scent of woodsmoke and decay, the chilling touch of something

inhuman, a voice – his mother's perhaps? – a
desperate, choked whisper lost in the
maelstrom of time. He'd buried these
fragments deep, choosing the numbness of
denial over the agonizing truth they
represented. But the forbidden world had
exhumed them, thrusting them into the harsh
light of reality, leaving him exposed and
vulnerable.

The weight of this buried past pressed
down on him, heavier than any physical
burden. He tried to rationalize it, to
compartmentalize his experiences, but the line
between past and present had blurred,
becoming a chaotic tapestry woven with
threads of terror and uncertainty. The scars on
his arms, the ragged gashes from the clawed
hands of the Shadow Beasts, were physical
manifestations of a deeper trauma – a wound
on his soul that ran far deeper than skin. They
pulsed with a dull ache, a constant reminder of
his brush with oblivion.

He traced the jagged lines with a
calloused finger, a familiar ritual that offered
fleeting comfort. Each scar told a story – a
desperate struggle for survival, a confrontation
with unimaginable horror, a glimpse into the

abyss of the forbidden realm. He remembered the chilling beauty of the Obsidian Mirror, its surface reflecting not just his own haunted gaze but a kaleidoscope of otherworldly landscapes and the distorted faces of ancient, malevolent beings. He remembered the horrifying metamorphosis of the creatures, the way their flesh shifted and contorted, defying the laws of nature and reason. He remembered the chilling realization that the gateway wasn't simply a rift in space but a reflection of something far more sinister: a tear in the fabric of reality itself.

The knowledge clung to him like the stench of decay, a suffocating weight that threatened to drown him in despair. He felt like a broken vessel, shattered by the forces he had unwittingly unleashed. The world he'd once known felt distant, unreal, replaced by a stark, nightmarish landscape that had seeped into his very being. Even the mundane tasks of everyday life - the clatter of dishes, the hum of the city - were tainted by an underlying sense of dread, a constant reminder of the horrors lurking just beyond the veil of reality.

He sought solace in the bottle, finding temporary oblivion in the fiery embrace of cheap whiskey. But even the numbing effects of alcohol couldn't fully erase the memories, couldn't silence the whispers that haunted his waking hours. The images replayed themselves in his mind, a grotesque, endless film reel of carnage and despair. The faces of his allies and enemies flickered before his eyes, each one a testament to the brutality of his journey. He saw the desperate hope in the eyes of those he'd failed to save, the cold, calculating malice of those he'd managed to destroy.

The guilt gnawed at him relentlessly, a venomous serpent coiling around his heart. He had sealed the primary gateway, yes, but at what cost? He'd inadvertently fractured reality, creating countless smaller fissures, leaving the mortal world vulnerable to future incursions. He'd emerged from the forbidden realm victorious, yet he felt utterly defeated. The weight of responsibility pressed down on him, suffocating him with the knowledge that he was the last line of defense, the solitary guardian against the encroaching darkness.

His solitude was a cruel torment. He pushed away those who tried to reach out to him, his heart barricaded behind walls of fear and self-loathing. The very act of human connection felt like a betrayal, a reminder of his own profound isolation. He yearned for companionship, for someone who could understand the horrors he'd witnessed, but the knowledge of the truth was too terrifying to share. Who could possibly comprehend the alien landscapes, the twisted creatures, the terrifying rituals he'd encountered? He feared that uttering the words would be like releasing the horrors themselves back into the world.

He found himself drawn to the old, abandoned church on the outskirts of town. Its crumbling stones and stained-glass windows, shattered and fragmented, mirrored the state of his own soul. He spent hours there, amidst the silent decay, attempting to find some semblance of peace. He'd sit in the shadowed pews, staring at the decaying altar, lost in the labyrinth of his memories. The church had become a sanctuary, a place where he could confront his demons without the fear of judgment or intrusion.

One evening, amidst the flickering candlelight, a flicker of memory surfaced – a memory so vivid, so real, that it felt like he was reliving it. He was a child, no older than five, standing in a dimly lit room, the air thick with the scent of incense and something else...something acrid and sickeningly sweet. A woman, her face obscured by shadow, was chanting in a language he didn't understand. He saw a symbol etched into the floor, a sigil radiating an unsettling energy. A sudden, sharp pain pierced his mind, and the memory fractured, leaving him gasping for breath.

The fragment, though incomplete, sent a jolt of recognition through him. It was the same symbol he'd seen etched into the Obsidian Mirror, a symbol that represented something ancient and profoundly evil. The realization struck him with the force of a physical blow: his past was inextricably linked to the forbidden world, to the ancient conspiracy that threatened humanity's existence. He wasn't just a victim; he was part of the story, a pawn in a game played by forces far older and more powerful than himself.

The weight of this revelation was immense, crushing him under the burden of his newfound knowledge. He felt a profound sense of dread, an understanding that his journey was far from over. The scars remained, not just physical reminders of his battles, but a roadmap to a future fraught with unimaginable danger. The battle for his soul, and for the fate of the mortal world, had only just begun. He was alone, scarred, and haunted, yet he knew, with a chilling certainty, that he had to continue fighting. He had to uncover the truth about his past, to understand the significance of the symbol, and to confront the forces that had drawn him into this terrifying maelstrom. The forbidden world might have been temporarily sealed, but the scars remained, a testament to the horrors he'd witnessed, and a grim prophecy of the darkness yet to come.

Chapter 9:

Whispers of the Abyss

The air hung heavy, thick with a silence that felt more oppressive than any scream. The victory, hard-won and bought with a terrible price, felt less like triumph and more like a temporary reprieve. Elias Thorne, his body a patchwork of scars – physical reminders of the abyss he'd wrestled with – stood on the precipice of the world he'd almost saved, yet the weight of what remained unsettled pressed down on him like a physical burden. He wasn't whole. He was a vessel, cracked and scarred, barely containing the horrors he'd witnessed.

The gateway, or what remained of it, was a fractured scar upon the fabric of reality. It wasn't sealed, not truly. The cataclysmic struggle had shattered it, splintering the connection between the mortal world and the forbidden realm, but it hadn't severed it entirely. Thin, almost imperceptible threads still clung to existence, whispering promises of resurgence, of a return to the nightmare he'd fought so desperately to contain. He felt them, sensed them as a constant, low hum of dread resonating in the very marrow of his bones. It was a subtle thing, a tremor in the air, a prickling on the skin, but to Elias, it was a deafening roar.

He'd seen the Architects of Despair, their forms grotesque parodies of godhood, their power fueled by an ancient and malignant corruption. He'd glimpsed the source of their strength, a festering wound in the heart of the abyss, a wellspring of pure, unadulterated malice. He'd driven a stake through their hearts, but it felt insufficient, a symbolic gesture against a cosmic evil that refused to truly die. The whispers confirmed his suspicions. They were not vanquished, only wounded. They were healing, gathering strength in the shadows, waiting.

The nights were the worst. The silence, once a welcome reprieve, became a breeding ground for fear. He'd find himself staring into the darkness, his heart hammering a frantic rhythm against his ribs, convinced he could feel the gaze of something unseen, something ancient and hungry, upon him. He'd see flickering shadows in his peripheral vision, hear rasping breaths in the dead of night, the echoes of the abyss clinging to the edges of his sanity. Sleep offered no respite; his dreams were a maelstrom of twisted landscapes and monstrous figures, a constant replay of the horrors he'd witnessed. His waking hours were little better, haunted by the chilling memories of his fallen allies, their sacrifices a heavy weight upon his conscience.

He wasn't alone in his apprehension. The few survivors, the ones who had escaped the carnage, felt it too. The air crackled with a palpable sense of unease. Even the creatures of the forbidden realm, those monstrous beings he'd fought alongside, seemed to be on edge, their senses heightened, sensing the approaching storm. There were subtle shifts in their behaviour, a nervous energy that mirrored his own. They sensed it, this looming threat, this insidious resurgence of darkness.

One such creature, a hulking monstrosity he'd named "Gorth," a being composed of shadows and razor-sharp claws, had approached him in the ravaged remains of the ancient city. Gorth, despite his monstrous appearance, had shown an unexpected loyalty, a begrudging respect forged in the crucible of battle. He communicated through a series of guttural growls and gestures, but Elias had learned to understand the nuances of his communication, to read the subtle shifts in his posture, the subtle tightening of his clawed hands. Gorth had touched Elias's arm, his shadowy hand surprisingly gentle, a silent acknowledgement of the shared danger.

"The whispers grow louder," Gorth had conveyed, his voice a low rumble that seemed to emanate from the very earth itself. The language was alien, but the sentiment was unmistakable. It was a warning, a grim acknowledgement of the imminent threat.

Over the following weeks, Elias found himself rebuilding his alliances. He discovered that the fragile peace he'd forged wasn't just limited to the human survivors. Many of the creatures of the forbidden realm, those who had been caught in the crossfire of the war between the Architects of Despair and the remnants of the ancient civilization, were wary of the encroaching darkness. Their motivations were complex, as were their alliances, but a common thread bound them together – a shared fear of the encroaching power that threatened to engulf them all.

He found allies in unexpected places. A tribe of winged, serpentine creatures, their scales shimmering with iridescent colors, offered their allegiance, their keen senses able to perceive the subtle shifts in the magical energies emanating from the fractured gateway. A solitary giant, his body composed of living rock and moss, offered his strength and ancient wisdom. He spoke of forgotten rituals, lost spells, ways of sensing the encroaching darkness, ways of combating it, even if they were desperate and dangerous measures.

Together, they began a slow, painstaking process of preparation. They scoured the ruins of the ancient city, searching for clues, for forgotten knowledge, for any means of strengthening their defenses. They learned to interpret the subtle shifts in the landscape, the way the wind howled, the subtle changes in the light, all of which spoke of the approaching storm. Elias, utilizing his newfound understanding of the forbidden realm's magic, worked tirelessly, using his knowledge of the gateway to develop strategies that would help to contain any future incursions.

He spent countless hours poring over the ancient texts, deciphering cryptic symbols and unraveling forgotten prophecies. He uncovered rituals, long since lost to time, which could potentially be used to disrupt the flow of the encroaching darkness. However, such rituals were perilous, requiring a sacrifice, a cost.

The whispers of the abyss grew louder, more insistent. There were subtle signs – a shifting of the earth, a change in the weather patterns, strange disturbances in the very fabric of reality. He felt it in the growing unease of his allies, in the tightening of their defenses. He felt it most acutely within himself, a rising tide of fear and apprehension that he struggled to keep at bay.

The old wounds, both physical and psychological, throbbed with a renewed intensity. He was haunted by the faces of the fallen, by the burden of their sacrifices, by the knowledge that he was, once again, standing on the precipice of a nightmare. He was no longer just Elias Thorne, the man haunted by a cryptic past. He was something more, something less. He was a warrior, scarred but unbowed, standing sentinel against an encroaching darkness that threatened to consume everything. He knew that the battle was far from over; the whispers of the abyss were a constant reminder of the storm that was brewing, and he stood ready, grim-faced and resolute, to meet it head-on. The game was afoot, the fight for survival was renewed. The true reckoning was still to come.

The flickering gaslight cast long, dancing shadows across the cobblestones, mirroring the unease that gnawed at Elias. The victory, so brutally hard-won, felt fragile, a thin veneer over a chasm of encroaching darkness. He'd sealed the gateway, or so he thought. The abyss hadn't been vanquished, merely contained, its malevolent whispers still echoing in the silence. He felt them, not as sounds, but as a pressure, a subtle shift in the very fabric of reality.

His hand instinctively went to the scar that bisected his left arm, a jagged reminder of the monstrous creature he'd slain in the heart of the abyss. The scar itched, a phantom pain that mirrored the disquiet in his soul. It wasn't just the physical wounds; his mind bore a deeper, more insidious trauma, etched with images of unimaginable horror. Sleep offered no solace, only a parade of grotesque visions, a nightmarish replay of the battles fought and the horrors witnessed.

He'd spent the days following the confrontation in a state of hyper-vigilance, his senses sharpened to an almost unbearable degree. The city, once a familiar refuge, now felt alien, a place teeming with unseen presences. The air thrummed with an unnatural energy, a low hum that resonated deep within his bones, a symphony of impending doom. His once-reliable instincts were now plagued by doubt, whispering insidious suggestions, echoing the whispers of the abyss.

The first sign came subtly, almost imperceptibly. A stray cat, its fur the colour of midnight, froze mid-stride, its back arched, its eyes wide with an unnatural terror. It stared intently at a seemingly empty alleyway before darting away with a panicked yelp. Elias dismissed it initially as mere animal instinct, a common occurrence in a city as old and grimy as this one. But the unease lingered, a persistent prickle at the back of his neck.

Then came the nightmares, more vivid, more visceral than ever before. He dreamt of vast, desolate landscapes, where twisted, skeletal trees clawed at a bruised sky. The creatures he'd faced in the abyss were present, but altered, more powerful, their forms shifting and reforming in ways that defied logic and anatomy. They moved with a chilling sentience, their eyes burning with a malevolent intelligence that chilled him to the marrow. The whispers in his dreams were no longer subtle; they were deafening, a cacophony of voices that spoke of a resurgence, a return to dominance.

He consulted the ancient grimoires he'd salvaged from the ruins of the forgotten city, hoping for some explanation, some clue. The texts spoke of cycles, of ebb and flow, of a power that slumbered but never truly died. They hinted at rituals, sacrifices, and a resurgence that would herald an age of unimaginable horror. The old prophecies spoke of signs, subtle indicators that would herald the return of the abyssal entities: the unsettling behaviour of animals, the distortion of shadows, the appearance of unnatural symbols in unexpected places.

Elias began to notice these signs, initially dismissed as coincidence, now growing in frequency and intensity. Shadows stretched and twisted, seeming to writhe and pulse with a life of their own. He saw strange symbols – glyphs he recognized from his study of the grimoires – etched into the walls of buildings, scratched into the cobblestones, seemingly appearing overnight. They were cryptic, ancient, and disturbingly beautiful, hinting at a ritualistic purpose.

He started seeing them everywhere; in the cracks in the walls, on the faded posters plastered on lampposts, even etched into the soot of a chimney. They were subtle, almost imperceptible, yet undeniably there, a malignant stain spread across the city's canvas. The more he saw, the more he realised the true extent of the invasion. It wasn't just a single entity attempting a return, but a coordinated effort, a vast, insidious conspiracy spanning centuries.

His investigations led him to the city's underbelly, a network of forgotten tunnels and sewers, where the city's darker secrets were kept. He discovered a clandestine society, a cult devoted to the abyssal entities, their rituals designed to weaken the barriers between worlds, to facilitate the return of their dark masters. The cult's members were diverse; from desperate outcasts to wealthy elites, all united by their shared desire for power and chaos. Their meetings were shrouded in secrecy, taking place in forgotten crypts and abandoned catacombs, places where the whispers of the abyss were amplified.

He witnessed one such ritual, a grotesque ceremony involving human sacrifice and incantations in a tongue older than the city itself. The air was thick with a cloying stench of decay and something else, something ancient and indescribably foul. He saw the entities emerge from the shadows, not as the monstrous beings he had encountered before, but as subtle, insidious corruptions, whispering promises of power and dominion.

The encounter left Elias shaken, his resolve tested. He was no longer fighting against a single, identifiable threat; he was facing a vast, interconnected network of insidious forces. The battle wasn't merely a physical one; it was a war of wills, a battle against the insidious power of belief and fear. The whispers of the abyss were no longer distant murmurs; they were a chorus, a deafening roar, attempting to break through the fragile barriers of reality.

The city was changing. The once familiar streets now felt like an ominous labyrinth, each shadow harboring a potential threat. He felt a constant sense of being watched, the weight of unseen eyes pressing down on him, adding to the burden of his already fractured psyche. The lines between reality and nightmare were blurring, the boundaries between the worlds growing increasingly porous. The nightmares had begun to bleed into his waking hours, fragments of his dreams lingering in the corners of his vision.

The whispers grew louder, not just in his ears but in his heart, a chilling chorus of promises and threats. The entities were not simply trying to regain power; they were attempting to corrupt him, to twist his will, to turn him into one of their instruments. He fought back, clinging to his sanity, his memories, his humanity. He knew that if he fell, the gateway would be breached, the abyss would consume everything.

The fight was far from over. The resurgence was underway. And Elias Thorne, scarred warrior, stood alone, on the precipice of an unthinkable horror, facing a battle that threatened to consume not just his soul, but the very fabric of reality itself. The whispers of the abyss were a constant reminder of the looming threat, a haunting prelude to the final, terrifying act. The true reckoning was at hand, and he would meet it, armed with nothing but his resolve, his dwindling sanity, and a desperate hope for survival in a world increasingly consumed by the shadows of a nightmare. The whispers promised dominion; he would fight to silence them.

The chill wind whipped through the skeletal remains of the abandoned church, carrying with it the scent of decay and the faint whisper of something ancient and malevolent. Elias huddled deeper into his threadbare coat, the rough wool doing little to ward off the gnawing cold that seeped into his bones, a cold that mirrored the icy dread that clung to his heart. He'd won a battle, yes, but the war was far from over. The abyss, though temporarily sealed, continued its insidious advance, its presence a suffocating weight upon the world.

He wasn't alone, not entirely. The faint glow of a lantern illuminated three figures huddled near a crumbling altar: Seraphina, her face etched with a grim determination that belied her frail appearance; Rhys, the grizzled hunter, his eyes burning with a cold fire; and a newcomer, a wizened old woman named

Maeve, her presence radiating an unnerving aura of ancient power. Maeve, a recluse whispered about in hushed tones in the darkest corners of the city, was a conduit, a link to the forgotten lore of a time before the abyss's encroachment.

"You summoned us, Thorne," Rhys stated, his voice a low growl, the words hanging heavy in the air. His weathered hands rested on the hilt of his hunting knife, a blade that had tasted the blood of countless creatures from the abyss. "What fresh hell do you require our aid in confronting?"

Elias, his gaze fixed on the flickering lantern flame, ran a hand through his grizzled hair. "The gateway is sealed, but only temporarily. The abyss is resilient, it seeks a way back. I need to prepare, to understand more about the forces at play, to...to fight back." His voice was raspy, strained from days of sleepless nights haunted by visions of the horrifying entities he'd faced.

Seraphina, ever the pragmatist, stepped forward. "What preparations are you suggesting, Elias? We are but three, against an enemy that seems boundless."

"Three is enough," Elias said, his voice strengthening with a renewed resolve. "Three with the knowledge and the resources we can gather. Maeve...she is the key. Her knowledge of ancient rituals, of the forgotten wards and defenses...it's our only hope."

Maeve remained silent, her eyes, ancient and knowing, fixed on Elias. She finally spoke, her voice a dry rasp, like leaves skittering across bare earth, "The whispers grow louder, child. The veil thins. The old gods stir in their slumber. They seek release." She gestured towards a hidden alcove behind the altar, revealing a collection of dusty tomes, strange symbols etched onto their leather-bound covers. "Within these pages lies the knowledge to combat the encroaching darkness. But be warned, the cost... it is high."

The following days were a blur of frantic activity. The abandoned church became their sanctuary, a place where they delved into Maeve's ancient texts, deciphering cryptic passages and arcane diagrams. Each page turned revealed a terrifying tapestry of forgotten lore, detailing the origins of the abyss, the rituals used to summon its horrors, and, most importantly, the defenses that might repel its advance.

The texts spoke of powerful wards, crafted from materials both earthly and otherworldly – bones of creatures from the abyss, rare herbs grown under the light of a dying star, and minerals mined from veins that ran deep within the earth. Gathering these components proved a daunting task, requiring perilous journeys into the shadowed corners of the city and beyond.

Rhys, with his years of experience tracking and hunting monstrous creatures, proved invaluable. He navigated the treacherous back alleys, sewers, and abandoned catacombs of the city, battling packs of monstrous vermin and avoiding the gaze of unseen horrors lurking in the darkness. He returned with strange bones, twisted and unnatural, that whispered tales of unimaginable cruelty and suffering.

Seraphina, though physically frail, possessed a remarkable gift for identifying and interpreting ancient symbols. She deciphered cryptic clues hidden within Maeve's texts, revealing locations of forgotten shrines and ancient burial grounds where the remaining herbs and minerals could be found. Her knowledge was instrumental, guiding them through ancient ruins and forgotten tunnels, where the air hung heavy with the scent of death and decay.

Elias, haunted by his past, found a sense of purpose in the perilous task. He channeled his grief, his anger, his terror, into a fierce determination to protect the world from the encroaching darkness. He unearthed ancient weapons, forgotten in forgotten temples, artifacts imbued with a power that resonated with his own nascent abilities.

Their collaboration forged a bond between them – a reluctant fellowship forged in the crucible of unimaginable fear and imminent danger. They learned to trust each other, relying on each other's strengths to overcome their individual weaknesses. Elias, the reluctant hero, found himself leading the group, his inherent leadership abilities emerging from the depths of his despair. He learned to delegate tasks, to trust Rhys's hunting prowess and Seraphina's scholarly insight, while relying on Maeve's ancient wisdom and guidance.

Yet, as they delved deeper into the ancient lore, they uncovered a horrifying truth – the abyss wasn't merely a gateway to another realm, but an entity of pure malevolence, a being of immense power that fed upon fear and despair. And they found something else even more terrifying: the abyss wasn't merely seeking to break through; it was already here, weaving its way into the fabric of their world, its influence subtly corrupting their minds and their souls.

The whispers, once a faint tremor in the darkness, now became a cacophony, a chorus of dread that echoed in their minds, feeding upon their deepest fears, their darkest desires. Elias felt it most keenly, the whispering promises of power, the seductive allure of joining the abyss, of becoming one with the darkness.

One night, as they worked late into the night, deciphering a particularly cryptic passage, Elias felt a sudden, sharp pang of doubt. The text, illuminated by the flickering lantern light, seemed to shift and writhe before his very eyes, the words transforming into grotesque images of unimaginable horror. He felt a pull, a seductive temptation to succumb to the darkness, to abandon his desperate fight against the inevitable.

He gasped, his breath catching in his throat. He could feel the whispering voices, their promises echoing in his mind, tempting him with the seductive power of the abyss.

Seraphina, ever watchful, saw the change in his eyes, the flicker of uncertainty, the hint of something dark and malevolent taking root within his soul. She placed a calming hand on his arm, her touch grounding him, pulling him back from the precipice of despair.

"Hold fast, Elias," she whispered, her voice firm and reassuring. "Do not yield. We are together in this. We will fight."

Rhys, ever vigilant, drew his knife, the cold steel gleaming in the dim light, a stark contrast to the encroaching darkness that threatened to consume them. Maeve, her eyes burning with a strange, ethereal light, began to chant, an ancient incantation resonating through the decaying church, a bulwark against the abyss's seductive whispers.

The struggle against the abyss's influence was far from over. But in their newfound alliance, in their shared fear and determination, Elias found a strength he never knew he possessed. They were ready. The final battle was approaching, and they would face it, together. The whispers of the abyss promised annihilation; they would fight to silence them, even if it meant sacrificing everything. The fight for the survival of their world was only just beginning.

The flickering candlelight cast long, dancing shadows across the rough-hewn table, illuminating Elias's grim face. The air hung thick with the scent of woodsmoke and something else... something acrid and unsettling, a lingering echo of the abyssal energies he'd wrestled with in the crumbling church. He traced the worn leather of his grimoire, its pages filled with arcane symbols and chilling descriptions of entities best left undisturbed. But undisturbed was a luxury he no longer possessed. The abyss had been temporarily sealed, but the victory felt fragile, a momentary reprieve in a war of unimaginable scale.

He knew, with a certainty that chilled him to the bone, that the entities would return. Their power was immense, their hunger insatiable. This wasn't a simple matter of sealing a crack in a wall; it was stemming a tide of primordial chaos, a struggle against forces that predated humanity itself. His preparation had to be meticulous, his strategy flawless, or the consequences would be catastrophic.

First, he needed to understand the enemy. His grimoire offered fragmented glimpses, cryptic hints woven into the ancient texts. He spent hours poring over the faded script, deciphering the arcane language, piecing together the fragmented knowledge. He learned about their hierarchies, their strengths, their weaknesses – subtle vulnerabilities hidden beneath layers of horrifying power. The entities weren't monolithic; they were a complex web of beings, each with its own agenda and methods, a hive mind of unimaginable malevolence coordinated by something far older, far more sinister.

The knowledge he gleaned was horrifying. He learned of rituals, sacrifices, and pacts made in the deepest recesses of the forbidden world. He discovered the entities' thirst for souls, their insatiable hunger for the life force of the mortal realm, their ability to manipulate and corrupt even the strongest wills. He saw chilling illustrations depicting their grotesque forms, their power manifested in ways that defied human comprehension. Their eyes, he noted, were often described as pits of pure, unadulterated darkness, devoid of any light or emotion. There was something intensely unsettling about that emptiness, a void that seemed to swallow the very essence of light.

He needed more than ancient texts; he needed practical knowledge, tactical understanding. He sought out allies, individuals with skills and abilities that could complement his own. He contacted the enigmatic Sister Agnes, a woman whose knowledge of the occult was surpassed only by her unwavering faith. She possessed ancient artifacts, relics of a forgotten order, capable of amplifying their defenses and potentially weakening the entities' influence. Her quiet resolve amidst the impending doom offered a beacon of hope in the encroaching darkness.

Then there was Kael, the grizzled hunter, a man whose life had been entwined with the abyss for far longer than Elias cared to know. Kael had faced these creatures before, tasted their horror firsthand, and survived. His experience was invaluable, a guide through the murky, treacherous waters of the forbidden world. His knowledge of the land, its hidden paths, and the entities' hunting grounds was crucial. He also possessed a unique set of tools and weapons forged in the fires of ancient forges, weapons imbued with enchantments designed to repel and harm these monstrous entities.

Their combined knowledge formed the foundation of Elias's strategy. He planned a multi-pronged attack, a series of coordinated actions designed to weaken the entities and prevent their full return. He'd use Sister Agnes' artifacts to create defensive barriers, fortified positions where they could withstand the initial assault. Kael would use his knowledge of the land to lead them to strategic positions, ensuring that they would be able to inflict maximum damage without falling prey to the entities' overwhelming power. And Elias, using his own newfound abilities and his understanding of the abyssal energies, would launch a direct assault on the heart of the

incursion, attempting to disrupt the entities'
connection to their forbidden world.

The plan was risky, bordering on
suicidal. The entities possessed overwhelming
power, their numbers legion. A single mistake,
a lapse in concentration, could lead to
annihilation. But there was no room for
caution, no time for hesitation. The fate of the
world rested on their shoulders. The whispers
of the abyss had grown louder, more insistent,
the shadows lengthening, the cold tightening
its grip. They were running out of time.

Elias spent days meticulously preparing.
He sharpened his weapons, weapons crafted
not only for the physical but also the spiritual
realm. He etched protective runes into the
worn leather of his armor, imbuing it with
wards against the abyssal energies. He studied
ancient texts, searching for weaknesses in the
entities' defenses, for vulnerabilities that they
could exploit. He practiced his spells,
perfecting his control over the chaotic energies
that flowed within him, channeling them into
powerful attacks. He honed his body to peak
condition, preparing for the physical rigors of
the coming battle. He knew that his endurance
would be tested to the limits, his resolve

pushed beyond anything he'd experienced before.

He also prepared himself mentally. The horrors he'd witnessed had left their mark, and the constant pressure of the impending doom threatened to overwhelm him. He sought solace in meditation, focusing his mind, strengthening his spirit. He faced his inner demons, confronting the painful memories, the guilt and self-doubt that threatened to consume him. The battle wouldn't just be against the entities; it would also be against his own inner turmoil. He needed to be resolute, calm under pressure, because even a moment of weakness could prove fatal.

The preparations were not limited to weapons and strategies. Elias understood that the entities thrived on chaos and fear. He worked to rally the remaining populace, to instill hope and courage in their hearts, to unite them against the common enemy. He spoke of the coming battle, not as a lament for their demise but as a call to arms, a final stand against the encroaching darkness. He painted a picture of resilience, of unity, of a world worth fighting for. His words, infused with the weight of his experiences, resonated with the people, a beacon of hope in a world teetering on the brink of oblivion.

The night before the final confrontation, Elias sat alone, the flickering candlelight casting grotesque shadows on the walls of his makeshift sanctuary. He reviewed his plans, meticulously checking each detail, ensuring everything was in place. He felt a profound sense of dread, a chilling premonition of the horrors to come. But beneath the fear, a flicker of defiance burned. He would not yield. He would not surrender. He would fight to the bitter end, even if it meant sacrificing everything. He had stared into the abyss, and it had stared back, and he had not flinched. The time for whispers was over. The time for action had arrived. The fate of humanity hung in the balance, and Elias Thorne, haunted and broken but unwavering in his resolve, would determine its destiny.

Elias's heart pounded erratically, mimicking the flickering of the candle's flame. The temporary sealing of the abyssal rift had bought them time, a precious commodity he knew wouldn't last. He felt it in the bone-deep chill that had settled over the city, in the unsettling silence that replaced the usual nocturnal cacophony. A storm was brewing, far more potent and terrifying than any physical tempest. It was a gathering of shadows, a coalescence of malevolent energies that promised devastation far beyond his worst nightmares.

He ran a trembling hand over the worn, leather-bound grimoire, its pages filled with the chilling testament to the entities he had inadvertently unleashed. Each symbol seemed to throb with a malevolent pulse, a silent scream echoing from the depths of the forbidden world. The archaic script, once merely a source of academic fascination, now felt like a personal condemnation, a grim roadmap to his own impending doom.

The whispers, once faint and easily dismissed, had grown into a deafening roar, a chorus of unseen horrors closing in. He could almost taste the bitterness of their malevolence, a metallic tang that coated his tongue and clung to the back of his throat. His senses, sharpened by the proximity to the abyss, were assaulted by a symphony of unseen movements, a subtle shifting of shadows that spoke of a vast, unseen army amassing in the darkness.

He wasn't alone in sensing this encroaching doom. The city felt different, suffocated by an unnatural stillness, heavy with a sense of foreboding. The usually vibrant marketplace, a chaotic symphony of sights and sounds, was now eerily deserted. The laughter and bustling commerce had been replaced by a hushed silence, broken only by the occasional, frantic scurry of fleeing rats—harbingers of impending catastrophe. Even the city's wretched denizens, accustomed to the grime and desperation of their existence, seemed to sense the impending horror. They moved with an unnerving quietness, their eyes wide and filled with a primordial fear that echoed Elias's own.

He had sealed the rift, but the abyssal energies hadn't simply vanished. They had retreated, yes, but only to gather strength, to reconstitute their forces, ready for a final, cataclysmic assault. The ritual, harrowing as it had been, was merely a temporary bandage on a festering wound. The true battle was yet to come, a confrontation that would determine the fate of not only the city, but perhaps humanity itself.

Elias found himself staring into the flickering candlelight, lost in contemplation of the unseen enemy. The entities that dwelled in the abyss weren't merely creatures of flesh and blood; they were embodiments of primal fears, manifestations of humanity's darkest impulses, magnified and distorted into grotesque parodies of existence. They were shadows made manifest, whispers given form, and their power grew from the collective dread of mankind.

He recalled the grotesque entities he had encountered - the writhing, shapeless horrors that defied description; the creatures born of nightmare, their forms a grotesque mockery of familiar things; the beings of pure shadow, their presence felt as a chilling absence in the fabric of reality. Each encounter had left a permanent scar on his soul, etching a chilling tableau of horror in the depths of his memory. These were not opponents to be met with steel and sorcery alone; this was a war against the very essence of fear itself.

His grimoire offered scant solace. The ancient texts, filled with cryptic warnings and chilling descriptions, only served to amplify his dread. The spells and incantations he had painstakingly deciphered, once seeming like tools of power, now felt inadequate against the sheer scale of the impending threat. He understood, with sickening clarity, that he was facing an enemy that transcended the limitations of mortal understanding.

He spent the remaining hours before dawn meticulously preparing, reviewing his strategy, reinforcing his defenses, and making peace with the stark reality of his situation. His makeshift sanctuary, once a place of refuge, now felt like a cage awaiting the inevitable. The city was quiet, still, waiting with bated breath, for the storm to break. The air crackled with an unnatural energy, the scent of ozone and brimstone heavy in the air, a tangible manifestation of the impending doom.

The silence was the worst part, heavier than the oppressive weight of the approaching storm. It was a silence pregnant with unseen horrors, teeming with the whispered promises of annihilation. It was a silence that spoke of a universe teeming with malevolent entities, a universe where the lines between reality and nightmare had blurred, where the boundaries between the living and the dead were permeable, where hope was a fragile thing easily extinguished by the cold breath of the abyss.

He sharpened his blades, each stroke a desperate plea against the overwhelming tide of darkness. He checked his supplies, his every action a ritualistic defense against the encroaching fear. He whispered incantations, ancient words of power that held the faintest glimmer of hope in the face of utter despair. Yet, with each passing moment, the growing sense of dread intensified, a monstrous wave threatening to engulf him completely.

He knew he was fighting a war on multiple fronts. There was the physical battle, the desperate struggle against the monstrous entities that threatened to consume the world. But there was also the internal war, the relentless battle against his own doubts and fears, against the gnawing despair that threatened to consume him from within. The abyss had not only threatened the physical world; it had sought to corrupt his very soul.

The memories of his past, long buried, clawed their way to the surface. Haunted by fragments of a life he barely remembered, a life touched by darkness and scarred by loss, Elias grappled with the demons within, mirroring the struggle against the external horrors. The abyss, it seemed, had a personal stake in his downfall, using his past to amplify his fears, to weaken his resolve.

He closed his eyes, seeking solace in the quiet of his own mind, but even there he found no respite. The whispers continued, insidious and relentless, weaving tales of betrayal, defeat, and despair. They played upon his deepest fears, magnifying his insecurities, feeding on his vulnerabilities. He fought against the encroaching darkness, desperate to maintain his grip on sanity, to hold onto the flickering ember of hope that remained.

As the first rays of dawn crept over the horizon, painting the sky in hues of blood orange and sickly yellow, the silence finally broke. But it wasn't the sound of wind or rain that shattered the stillness, it was the sound of movement, a vast and terrifying rustling that sent shivers down Elias's spine. The storm had arrived. The whispers had given way to a horrifying cacophony, a symphony of screams and groans echoing from the unseen legions massing beyond the city walls. The gathering storm had become a raging tempest, and Elias

Thorne, haunted and broken, but unyielding, stood ready to face the coming darkness. The fight for humanity's survival had begun. And this time, there would be no reprieve.

Chapter 10:

A Chilling Resonance

The wind howled a mournful dirge
through the skeletal remains of what was once
a vibrant forest, its branches clawing at the
bruised, twilight sky. The air hung heavy with
the stench of decay and something else,
something ancient and indescribably foul – a
lingering echo of the abyss Elias had fought so
hard to seal. He stood on the precipice, gazing
down into the chasm that had once been the
gateway, a wound in the fabric of reality. It
wasn't completely closed. Not entirely.

A faint, pulsating luminescence
emanated from the depths, a sickly green light
that writhed and shifted like a living thing. It
was a subtle tremor, a barely perceptible ripple
in the air, but to Elias, it was a scream, a
chilling reminder of the horrors he'd faced and
the precarious peace he'd managed to forge.
The battle had left its mark, not just on the
landscape, but on his soul. He carried the
weight of countless deaths, the ghosts of his
fallen allies clinging to him like shadows.

His hands, once delicate and refined,
were now scarred and calloused, a testament to
the brutal struggle. Each scar told a story, a
grim chronicle of close calls and desperate acts
of survival. He ran a calloused thumb over the

jagged line that bisected his left palm, a souvenir from his encounter with the obsidian behemoth that guarded the heart of the abyss. The memory of its cold, lifeless eyes still haunted his dreams, a chilling vision that refused to fade.

The physical wounds were nothing compared to the psychic scars. The glimpse into the abyss had shattered his perception of reality, revealing a terrifying truth about the universe's fragility and the malevolent forces that lurked just beyond the veil of human understanding. He'd seen things that defied description, things that gnawed at the edges of sanity, leaving him with a profound sense of unease that no amount of sleep or solace could erase. He was a changed man, forever altered by his descent into darkness.

His transformation wasn't just physical or psychological; it was spiritual. He'd crossed a threshold, traversed a boundary that no man should ever cross, and emerged on the other side, a reluctant hero bearing the burden of a world he'd saved, yet one that remained teetering on the brink of destruction. He carried the weight of responsibility for a world barely clinging to its sanity, the constant, subtle threat of the abyss never far from his mind.

He'd gone into the abyss a man haunted by his past, his memories fragmented and shrouded in mystery. Now, he understood the truth. His past was inextricably linked to the forbidden realm, to the ancient conflict, and to the gateway itself. His lineage was cursed, tied to the entities that sought to conquer the mortal world, a cruel twist of fate that had thrust him into the role of reluctant savior.

The memories, once fragmented, now coalesced into a terrifying tapestry. He remembered the whispers in the dark, the spectral figures flitting at the periphery of his vision, the cold, clammy touch of the ancient artifact that had opened the gateway. He remembered his ancestors, their shadowed figures, their whispered incantations, and the unholy pact that bound them to the forces of darkness. This revelation was a fresh wound on top of the many he already bore. It was a curse passed down through generations, a legacy of darkness that he, despite everything, had somehow managed to break.

The lingering glow from the chasm pulsed again, a stronger beat this time. Elias felt a cold dread creeping up his spine, a primal fear that transcended logic and reason. The gateway wasn't merely unsealed; it was awakening. The subtle tremors in the air were intensifying, and he could hear a faint, guttural chanting emanating from the depths – a chorus of monstrous voices, a symphony of impending doom.

He wasn't alone. In the distance, he saw figures emerging from the shadows of the ruined forest. They were survivors, like him, scarred and changed by their experience in the abyss. Their faces were etched with a mixture of fear and grim determination, their eyes reflecting the chilling resonance of the unsealed gateway. They were bound together, not by friendship or kinship, but by a shared trauma and the unspoken understanding of what lay before them.

This uneasy alliance, forged in the crucible of the abyss, was their only hope. They were the last line of defense between humanity and the encroaching darkness, a fragile shield against the tide of monstrous creatures and malevolent forces waiting to spill forth from the newly awakened gateway. The fight wasn't over. In fact, it had only just begun.

The weight of responsibility pressed down on Elias like a physical burden. He was not a hero, not in the traditional sense. He was a broken man, burdened with a cursed lineage and haunted by memories he couldn't escape. Yet, he was the only one who could stand against the encroaching darkness, the only one who could face the nightmares that crawled from the depths of the abyss.

As the first tendrils of monstrous shadows began to slither from the gateway, Elias knew that he couldn't rest. He had sealed the wound, but he had not healed it. The abyss still whispered, beckoning him back to its depths, its siren song a constant reminder of the fragility of their victory. The subtle tremor beneath his feet intensified, becoming a distinct quake that shook the very foundations of the scarred earth. It was a warning, a chilling resonance echoing the impending doom that threatened to engulf them all. The fight to keep the gateway closed, to safeguard the human world, had just become far more terrifying. The battle for survival was far from over.

The subtle shifts in the ground beneath Elias's feet became more pronounced, the earth groaning under the strain of some immense, unseen pressure. The faint green luminescence from the gateway intensified, casting an eerie, otherworldly glow on the surrounding ruins. The air crackled with a palpable energy, the very fabric of reality seeming to fray at the edges. He could feel it now, the insidious presence of the entities drawing closer, feeling their malignant energy, sensing their malevolent intent. They were regaining their power.

He glanced at his companions, their faces grim, reflecting the same unspoken fear. Each of them carried their own burdens, their own scars, their own memories of the horrors they'd witnessed. They were a band of survivors, bound together by a shared trauma and a desperate desire to prevent the utter annihilation of their world. Yet, a chilling sense of foreboding hung heavy in the air, a palpable sense of helplessness in the face of the overwhelming power of the abyss.

Elias knew that the fragile peace they'd secured was only temporary, a mere respite before the next onslaught. The gateway may have been partially sealed, but it was not closed, and the entities were far from defeated. This was only the beginning of a long, brutal war, a war that would test their courage, their resilience, and their very souls. Their victory had been pyrrhic, a temporary reprieve bought at an unimaginable cost.

The darkness was returning, not with a roar, but with a subtle whisper, a chilling resonance that slithered into their minds, their hearts, their souls. The fight to protect humanity was far from over, and the weight of that responsibility crushed Elias with a renewed sense of dread. He looked down at the pulsating green light emanating from the depths of the chasm, his eyes reflecting the grim determination etched onto his scarred face. The unsealed gateway was a constant reminder of the precarious balance between worlds, a chilling testament to the unending war between light and darkness, a war in which he was now forever entangled.

The epilogue didn't offer closure, but a chilling promise of what was yet to come. The forbidden worlds, once seemingly contained, were now stirring. Elias, despite his heroism, was left with the haunting knowledge that the fight was far from over, the victory hard-won and tenuous. He was a changed man, irrevocably marked by his experiences, forever bound to the fate of a world perpetually threatened by the unimaginable horrors that lurked beyond the veil. The abyss had opened a door, and it was Elias's burden to prevent its ultimate conquest. The lingering resonance of the unsealed gateway served not as an ending but a stark, chilling beginning. The readers are left with the unsettling feeling of an ongoing threat, a pervasive sense of dread that clings to the air, a promise of more darkness yet to come. The story ends, not with a triumphant resolution, but with the quiet, unsettling recognition that the fight for survival is unending, and the shadow of the abyss will forever loom large.

The wind, a keening banshee, whipped at Elias's cloak, the tattered remnants of a life he barely recognized. He stood at the edge of the chasm, the air thick with the coppery tang of blood, both his own and... something else. Something ancient, something alien. The gateway, the gaping maw that had spat forth horrors beyond comprehension, was mostly sealed, but not entirely. A thin, pulsating fissure remained, a malevolent eye staring out from the earth's scarred skin. The victory, hard-fought and bloody, felt hollow, a pyrrhic triumph at best.

He traced the jagged edges of the fissure with a trembling hand, his fingers brushing against a viscous, oily substance that seemed to writhe beneath his touch. It smelled of sulfur and decay, a scent that clung to his memory like a shroud. The experience had seared itself into his very being, transforming him from a man haunted by shadows into something... different. He wasn't sure what he was anymore. A hero? A monster? The line had blurred, vanished entirely, lost in the swirling chaos of the forbidden worlds.

His reflection in the shimmering, oily surface of the fissure was a stranger. His eyes, once a clear, almost innocent blue, now held a depth of shadowed knowing, a chilling wisdom born of witnessing unimaginable horrors. Lines etched themselves deep into his face, the roadmap of his ordeal, a testament to the battles fought and won, and the scars that wouldn't heal. His hands, calloused and scarred, bore the marks of desperate struggles, of clinging to life against overwhelming odds.

He was etched with the very landscape he had fought to save.

The transformation hadn't been merely physical. It ran deeper, twisting into the very fabric of his soul. He remembered the fear, the bone-chilling terror that had gripped him in the face of the abyss. He remembered the sickening crunch of bone, the screams that echoed still in his ears, long after they had faded into the wind. He remembered the betrayal, the agonizing choices that had cost him dearly, the weight of sacrifices made in the face of oblivion. And he remembered the things he had done to survive, things that stained his conscience like an indelible ink.

The memories, once fragmented and shadowy, now coalesced into a horrifying tapestry woven from darkness and despair. He saw himself in the distorted reflection of the fissure—not as a hero, but as a reluctant participant in a cosmic horror story, a pawn in a game played by entities far older and more powerful than himself. He was a survivor, yes, but survival had come at a terrible price.

He felt a kinship with the creatures he had fought, a twisted empathy born from shared suffering. He understood their hunger, their desperate clinging to existence in a world that sought to erase them. He understood their pain, the agony of being hunted, of being hunted as he had been. He was no longer separate; he was woven into the very fabric of this nightmarish realm.

The chilling resonance of the abyss pulsed within him, a constant, throbbing reminder of the horrors he had faced. It was a physical presence, a constant weight in his chest, a cold dread that snaked through his veins. He carried the abyss within him, a dark echo of the world beyond the veil. Sleep was a battlefield, haunted by grotesque visions and the screams of the damned. His dreams were no longer dreams, but nightmarish reflections of the horrors he had witnessed, a terrifying replay of his journey into the heart of darkness.

His days were filled with a gnawing anxiety, a constant vigilance against an unseen enemy. The world had shifted, subtly, imperceptibly, but the change was there. There was a new tension in the air, a subtle shift in the balance of power. He felt it in the uneasy silence of the forests, in the watchful eyes of the townspeople who regarded him with a mixture of awe and fear. They knew. They sensed what he carried within him. They sensed the darkness that clung to him like a second skin.

His solitude was a cage. He sought to distance himself from those he cared for, afraid of tainting them with the darkness that consumed him. Yet, he was surrounded by it, encased in it, a prisoner in the heart of his own transformation. The shadows of the abyss followed him, not just in his mind, but in the real world. He saw glimpses of movement at the edge of his vision, sensed a malevolent presence lurking in the periphery. He felt a constant, chilling pressure on his skin, the unnatural weight of something ancient and evil, watching, waiting.

He tried to find solace in the mundane, but even the simple act of eating brought a surge of nausea. The taste of food was foul, a grotesque parody of nourishment, reminding him of the grotesque feasts of the creatures from the abyss. The sun felt harsh on his skin, a reminder of the blinding light of the forbidden realms. Even the sound of rain was distorted, a percussive rhythm that echoed the chaotic symphony of the abyss.

He found himself drawn to the chasm, to the lingering fissure that was a constant, throbbing reminder of his failure to completely seal the gateway. He would stand for hours, gazing into the darkness, searching for any sign of movement, of a new breach. The anticipation was a visceral pain, a constant tension that left him drained and exhausted. He was waiting, waiting for the inevitable.

He knew, with a certainty that chilled him to the bone, that the fight was far from over. The creatures of the abyss were not defeated; they were merely slumbering, gathering strength, waiting for their moment to return. And Elias, the reluctant hero, was their unwilling guardian, forever bound to the fate of the world, forever burdened by the horrors he had witnessed, forever marked by the darkness that clung to him like a shroud. He was a walking paradox, a hero bearing the scars of a monster.

He was no longer a man haunted by his past; he was a man possessed by it. The transformation was complete, but the journey was far from over. The chilling resonance of the abyss echoed not only in the fissure, but within him, a constant, unrelenting pulse that would beat until the final, inevitable confrontation. The world he knew, the world he had struggled to save, was changed irrevocably. And the darkness that had been held at bay now threatened to consume all. The seeds of oblivion had been sown, and only time would tell if he, the reluctant guardian, could prevent the ultimate harvest. The fight for the soul of humanity had begun anew, and it was a battle that would be fought not only in the physical realm, but also within the deepest, darkest corners of his soul. The abyss had claimed him, body and soul, and the price of survival was a life forever tainted by darkness, an eternal vigil against the looming return of the creatures of nightmares. His victory was a mere reprieve, a brief respite before the next, more terrible onslaught. The silence of the world was deceptive; a pregnant silence that hinted at the horrors yet to come, a grim prelude to the inevitable.

The acrid smell of sulfur clung to Elias like a shroud, a constant reminder of the chasm's lingering breath. The fissure, a jagged scar upon the earth, pulsed with an unnatural luminescence, a malevolent heartbeat echoing the disquiet in his own chest. He'd sealed the gateway, or so he thought. The victory had

been bought with blood and sacrifice, a
harrowing dance with oblivion that had left
him irrevocably changed. The faces of the
fallen flickered behind his eyelids – the stoic
determination of Kael, the haunted eyes of
Lyra, the chilling final smile of the
Necromancer, a twisted parody of triumph.
He'd saved the world, but at what cost?

He ran a hand over the crudely
fashioned amulet hanging around his neck, the
cold metal a stark contrast to the feverish heat
beneath his skin. The artifact, once a key to
unimaginable horrors, now felt like a weight, a
constant reminder of the power he'd wielded,
the darkness he'd touched. The power hadn't
left him; it had become a part of him, a
symbiotic relationship forged in the fires of the
abyss. He felt it now, a low thrumming in his
bones, a constant undercurrent of something
ancient and malevolent. It was a chilling
resonance, a grim echo of the forbidden realm
that clung to him like the shadow of a wraith.

Sleep offered no respite. His dreams
were a tapestry woven from nightmares –
grotesque creatures with eyes that burned like
coals, landscapes of twisted bone and shadow,
the unending shriek of the abyss. He woke

drenched in sweat, his heart pounding a frantic rhythm against his ribs, the taste of ash and despair lingering on his tongue. The days were little better. The world, once vibrant and full of life, now felt muted, drained of its color, its joy replaced by a pervasive sense of unease. Even the sunlight seemed to hold a sinister quality, as if the very essence of the world had been tainted.

He found himself drawn to the fissure, compelled by an unseen force, a morbid curiosity that whispered promises of oblivion. He'd stand for hours, gazing into the pulsating crack, feeling the abyss's insidious influence seeping into his very soul. He could almost hear the whispers, the insidious murmurings of forgotten gods and monstrous entities, promises of power and vengeance. He fought against it, against the seductive lure of the darkness, but the battle was exhausting, a constant war waged within the confines of his own mind.

The villagers, once grateful, now regarded him with a mixture of awe and fear. They saw him as a savior, a man who had wrestled with demons and emerged victorious, but also as something... other. He was no longer one of them. He carried the mark of the abyss, a brand of darkness that set him apart, making him both revered and feared. Their whispers followed him like shadows, their eyes full of a mixture of gratitude and apprehension. He was a hero, yes, but a hero tarnished by the darkness he'd confronted.

The physical wounds had healed, but the mental scars remained, deep and festering. The memories of the horrors he'd witnessed haunted him, the gruesome images replaying in his mind like a broken film reel. The faces of the creatures, their chilling cries, the sheer, unadulterated evil that radiated from them – it all clung to him, a grotesque tapestry woven into the very fabric of his being. He tried to find solace in solitude, but even the silence was filled with the chilling resonance of the abyss.

One night, under the cold gaze of a blood-red moon, he felt it – a shift in the earth, a subtle tremor that sent a shiver down his spine. The fissure pulsed with renewed intensity, the luminescence growing brighter, more menacing. He felt a pull, a gravitational force drawing him towards the chasm, a siren song of oblivion. He resisted, his will battling against the irresistible allure of the abyss. His muscles strained, his body trembling with the exertion, but the pull was relentless, unrelenting.

He fought back with every ounce of his being, his mind a battlefield where light and darkness clashed. The memories of his loved ones, the faces of the villagers he'd sworn to protect, fueled his resolve. He clung to the edges of sanity, his grip weakening with each passing moment. The abyss threatened to consume him, to drag him down into its eternal night.

He screamed, a primal sound ripped from the depths of his soul, a desperate plea against the encroaching darkness. The air crackled with energy, the ground beneath his feet vibrating with the power of the abyss. He could feel the monstrous entities stirring, their presence a palpable weight in the air, their whispers growing louder, more insistent.

Suddenly, the amulet around his neck grew warm, pulsing with a counter-force to the abyss's pull. It resonated with a strange, otherworldly energy, a beacon of light in the encroaching darkness. The pull weakened, slowly, gradually, but surely. He was not yet free, but he had bought himself time, a small reprieve in the unending war against the abyss.

He stumbled back, collapsing to his knees, his body drenched in sweat, his breath ragged and shallow. The amulet, once a symbol of his descent into darkness, now felt like a lifeline, a fragile connection to the world of the living. But the chilling resonance of the abyss remained, a constant reminder of the enduring threat, a testament to the horrors he'd faced and the battles yet to come. He knew, with a certainty that chilled him to the bone, that this was not the end, but merely a pause in the ceaseless struggle against the encroaching darkness. The forbidden realm still whispered, its voice a low, ominous hum in the silence of the night, promising a return, a reckoning that would shake the very foundations of reality. The fight was far from over; it was just beginning. The victory was fleeting, a temporary respite before the next, inevitable assault from the realms beyond. The world, and Elias himself, remained forever changed, forever marked by the chilling resonance of the abyss. The silence held a new meaning now, a heavy, pregnant silence that spoke of the horrors to come, a grim prelude to a future shrouded in shadow. He was the guardian, a reluctant champion against an ancient evil. And even as the first rays of dawn painted the eastern sky, the threat remained, a cold, ever-present shadow lurking at the edge of reality. The darkness waited. And Elias waited with it.

The dawn, when it finally broke, offered little solace. The sky, a bruised purple and sickly orange, mirrored the turmoil within Elias. He remained kneeling by the fissure, the amulet cold against his skin, its intricate carvings seeming to writhe in the nascent light. The air, though cleansed of the sulfurous stench, still hummed with an unsettling energy, a phantom vibration that resonated deep within his bones. The silence, once heavy with dread, now felt brittle, like a thin sheet of ice poised over a bottomless abyss.

He knew, with a chilling certainty, that the seal he'd placed on the gateway was not absolute. It was a temporary dam against a raging torrent, a fragile barrier against an ancient, unyielding power. The creatures of the forbidden realm, the grotesque horrors he'd battled, were not simply vanquished; they were driven back, their malevolence forced to

retreat, but not extinguished. Their essence,
like a persistent stain, remained.

The whispers, once confined to the
chasm, now seemed to emanate from the very
fabric of reality. He heard them in the rustling
leaves, in the creak of the ancient trees, in the
beating of his own heart. They spoke of a vast,
interconnected network of forbidden realms, a
multidimensional tapestry of darkness woven
from nightmares and ancient grudges. They
spoke of entities far older and more powerful
than the Necromancer, entities whose very
existence defied human comprehension.

His experiences had etched themselves
into his soul, leaving him a changed man. The
horrors he'd witnessed, the choices he'd made,
had irrevocably altered his perception of the
world, leaving him with a profound sense of
unease and a chilling premonition of future
conflict. The line between sanity and madness
had blurred, the weight of his burden pressing
down on him with the crushing force of a
thousand nightmares. Sleep offered no respite;
his dreams were haunted by the twisted faces
of the fallen, the chilling echoes of their
screams, the cold, reptilian gaze of the
creatures from beyond.

His physical wounds were healing, but the psychic scars ran deeper, festering beneath the surface of his consciousness. He felt a profound isolation, a chasm between himself and the world of the living. Even those who had witnessed the horror alongside him—those who had survived—could not fully comprehend the depths of his experience. He was alone in his knowledge, in his burden. He was the keeper of a terrible secret, a sentinel guarding against an unseen, ever-present threat.

He rose, his movements stiff and hesitant, his body still trembling from the ordeal. The amulet felt heavier now, a tangible manifestation of the weight of his responsibility. He looked out across the ravaged landscape, the earth scarred and broken, a testament to the battle that had just concluded. The silence was broken only by the distant cry of a bird, a lonely sound in the desolate expanse. He wasn't just protecting humanity; he was guarding against the unraveling of reality itself. The very fabric of existence seemed fragile, stretched thin by the incursions from the forbidden worlds.

Days turned into weeks, weeks into months. Elias, driven by a grim determination, began to investigate the ancient texts and artifacts he had recovered from the Necromancer's lair. The knowledge they contained was fragmented, cryptic, laced with allusions to forgotten rituals and powerful entities beyond human comprehension. He pieced together fragments of a lost history, a history of conflict between humanity and the inhabitants of the forbidden realms, a conflict that spanned millennia. He learned of powerful artifacts, of hidden gateways, of ancient prophecies foretelling a cataclysmic event—a final reckoning.

He discovered that the Necromancer had been merely a pawn in a much larger game, a puppet controlled by forces beyond his understanding. The entities residing in the forbidden realms were not unified; they were divided into warring factions, each vying for dominance, each possessing its own terrifying agenda. The conflict that Elias had witnessed was not an isolated incident; it was merely a prelude to a much larger, more devastating war. The seeds of future conflicts were sown, each promising even greater destruction than what he had already witnessed.

His research also revealed the existence of other individuals aware of the forbidden realms, individuals who possessed knowledge and power that rivaled his own. Some were benevolent, dedicated to protecting humanity from the encroaching darkness; others were consumed by ambition and a thirst for power, seeking to exploit the forbidden realms for their own nefarious ends. These individuals—some hidden within the shadows of society, others openly wielding their influence—were a new and unforeseen complication to the war against the encroaching darkness.

He found a hidden passage in an ancient library, concealed beneath layers of dust and cobwebs, a secret compartment revealing maps and scrolls detailing the network of gateways to other forbidden realms. Each location marked on these maps held a different level of threat, a different species of horror lurking beyond the veil. One map detailed the location of a realm inhabited by beings of pure shadow, entities capable of manipulating fear and despair, of twisting the human mind until it shattered. Another revealed a forgotten city, swallowed by the earth millennia ago, where monstrous creatures of unimaginable power slumbered, awaiting the opportune moment to rise and wreak havoc.

The more he learned, the more he realized the staggering scale of the threat. The fight against the creatures of the forbidden realm was only one aspect of a larger, more intricate struggle. There were political machinations, conspiracies spanning centuries, secret societies dedicated to the worship of ancient entities, and the ongoing threat of a devastating cataclysm. He was but one man, a small player in a much larger game with terrifying stakes.

The amulet pulsed faintly in his hand, a beacon in the gathering storm, a symbol of the weight of responsibility he now bore. He was no longer just a survivor; he was a reluctant leader, a guardian against a myriad of threats. His past, once a haunting presence, now provided him with a grim determination, a stark reminder of the price of inaction. He knew, with absolute certainty, that the chilling resonance of the abyss was not a temporary phenomenon; it was a constant, a prelude to the conflicts to come. He had sealed one gateway, but countless others remained, waiting to be opened, waiting to unleash even greater horrors upon the world. The war was far from over; the fight had just begun, a relentless and terrifying battle against the encroaching darkness, a battle he was determined to fight, even if it meant facing oblivion itself. The seeds of future conflicts were deeply planted, and only time would tell whether he could stop their terrifying growth. The darkness waited, and Elias, weary but resolute, waited with it, the future a terrifying yet compelling mystery.

The weeks that followed were a blur of frantic activity, a desperate scramble against the encroaching tide of darkness. Elias, despite his exhaustion, found a grim purpose in his newfound role. He wasn't a hero, not in the traditional sense. He was a man forced into a position he never wanted, a reluctant warden against a nightmare he barely understood. He established a clandestine network, recruiting individuals from the fringes of society—ex-military personnel haunted by their past, disgraced academics with knowledge of forgotten lore, and even a few individuals who, like him, bore the scars of encounters with the abyss.

Their base of operations was a crumbling manor house nestled deep within a forgotten forest, a place shrouded in its own eerie history, a fitting location for their grim task. The walls seemed to whisper secrets, the shadows to dance with unseen entities, a constant reminder of the precariousness of their existence. Each member of this ragtag group carried their own burdens, their own demons; a shared trauma that bound them together in their fight against the encroaching darkness. Their conversations were often punctuated by nervous laughter and uneasy silences, the weight of their collective knowledge pressing down on them like a physical burden.

Their research was a descent into madness, a relentless pursuit of knowledge that chipped away at their sanity. They studied ancient texts, deciphered cryptic symbols, and pieced together fragments of a horrifying truth about the forbidden worlds – worlds that weren't just parallel realities, but parasitic entities feeding off the life force of our own. They discovered that the fissure Elias had sealed was just one of many, scattered across the globe, each a potential gateway for the invasion. The amulet, they learned, was not merely a key; it was a conduit, a focal point for the energies that held the gateways shut. Its power was finite, and they were running out of time.

One particularly harrowing night, a storm of unnatural intensity raged outside, mirroring the tempest within their ranks. Dr. Albright, a brilliant but increasingly unstable historian, presented his findings about a ritual, an ancient ceremony that could permanently seal all gateways. The ritual, however, required a sacrifice—a life force of immense power to act as a binding agent. The room fell silent, the weight of the proposal heavy in the air. The faces of his companions, etched with worry and exhaustion, were illuminated by the flickering candlelight, casting grotesque shadows on the walls. The very air crackled with tension.

Elias felt the cold dread grip his heart. The thought of sacrifice, of condemning someone to death, felt abhorrent. Yet, the alternative – the complete annihilation of humanity – was a far more terrifying prospect. He looked at the faces of his companions, each one a reflection of his own internal struggle. Their collective silence spoke volumes; each weighing the horrifying choice. The silence stretched, each second echoing in the dimly lit room. The storm outside raged relentlessly, the wind howling like a banshee, as if echoing the turmoil within their souls.

Days bled into nights as they meticulously planned the ritual. The process was fraught with danger, requiring them to venture into ever more perilous territories, risking encounters with the creatures that lurked in the shadows. One expedition resulted in the loss of two of their team, their sacrifices a grim reminder of the stakes. The survivors pushed onward, the weight of their losses fueling their determination. The closer they got to achieving their goal, the more the abyss seemed to fight back, throwing more formidable obstacles in their path.

The final confrontation took place in the heart of a forgotten temple, a place of immense power and ancient evil. They battled grotesque creatures, abominations born from nightmares, their forms twisted and corrupted, their attacks brutal and relentless. The air vibrated with dark energy, the very stones seeming to writhe in pain under the onslaught. One by one, Elias and his companions fell, their wounds festering with a dark magic that defied healing. Yet, they persevered, driven by a desperate hope and an unwavering resolve.

The ritual itself was a terrifying ordeal. The air crackled with energy, the temple shaking under the strain. Elias, weakened but resolute, stood before the ancient altar, the amulet pulsating in his hand, its light a beacon in the encroaching darkness. He felt a presence, a malevolent force, pushing against him, trying to tear him apart. He held firm, his resolve forged in the crucible of his ordeal. The chanting echoed through the temple, a desperate plea against oblivion. The air grew thick with power, a tangible force that pressed down on them, threatening to crush them.

The final moments were a blur of intense energy, the temple convulsed in a cataclysmic eruption. Elias felt a searing pain, a tearing sensation as the energy coursed through his body. He saw visions—flashing images of the forbidden worlds, of the creatures they had fought, of the immense power they had unleashed. He felt the life force drain from him, a slow, agonizing process, leaving him on the brink of death.

When the chaos subsided, a profound silence descended. The temple, once a monument to ancient evil, now stood as a testament to their sacrifice. The abyss was silenced, the gateways sealed. Elias lay amongst the ruins, barely alive, his body ravaged, his spirit broken. His companions were gone, their sacrifice a grim price for humanity's survival.

But even in his weakened state, Elias felt a strange sense of peace. He had done what he had to do. The darkness that threatened the world had been pushed back, for now. He lay there, the amulet clutched tightly in his hand, its power depleted, but its presence still a symbol of the battles fought, the sacrifices made, and the resilience of the human spirit in the face of unimaginable horrors. The lingering resonance of the abyss remained—a chilling reminder of what lurked beneath the surface of reality, a constant threat that could return at any moment. But for now, there was silence, a fragile peace born from the ashes of a terrible war. The lingering questions about his past, the mysteries of the forbidden worlds remained, but there was little energy left in him to deal with them. He knew that the fight wasn't over, that the abyss would undoubtedly seek its vengeance. Yet, he had bought humanity time—a precious commodity in their struggle against the encroaching darkness. He closed his eyes, the weight of his ordeal pressing down on him, the chilling resonance a constant, albeit subdued, companion. The world was safe, for now. But the lingering shadow of the abyss, and the chilling resonance of what he had witnessed, would haunt him for the rest of his days. The cost of salvation was heavy, leaving a lasting impression etched not just on the landscape but also on his soul. The silence, while welcome, felt fragile, a thin veil over a still-roiling abyss, constantly reminding him of the precarious victory.

Epilogue

The wind howled through the broken landscape, carrying with it the scent of ash and something darker—something ancient. Elias stood at the precipice of the abyss, his gaze fixed on the faint glow seeping from the fissure below. The air shimmered with a faint, unnatural pulse, like the flicker of a dying heartbeat. He had seen the gateway close, seen the malevolence recoil back into the void, but a thin crack remained—a splinter of darkness still wedged into the skin of reality.

The victory they had fought so hard to achieve felt hollow. The gateway was sealed, but not entirely. A wound, still bleeding in slow, deliberate pulses, remained etched into the earth. Somewhere in the distance, the ruins of the once-mighty citadel stood silent and broken. His companions—Lyra, Orin, Damaris—were gone. Their faces haunted him, their voices echoing in the space between his breaths, their sacrifices etched into his soul as indelibly as the scars on his body.

He knelt, pressing his palm against the fissure's edge. The oily residue that lined the crack writhed under his touch, alive, sentient, and hungry. It recoiled, hissing silently, but it did not retreat entirely. They had stopped something terrible, something vast and insurmountable, but they had not destroyed it. They had bought time, nothing more. And time, Elias realized, was a fragile currency in a world that teetered on the edge of annihilation.

The weight of the artifact still hung around his neck. It was cold now, inert, as though the energy within it had been spent entirely. Yet, even in its silence, he could feel it there, watching. Waiting. He closed his eyes briefly, listening to the wind. It carried no whispers now, no monstrous voices slithering into his mind, but he could still feel them—out there, somewhere, just beyond the veil.

When Elias finally turned away from the fissure, the world seemed impossibly quiet. The sky above, bruised and streaked with fading twilight, offered no solace. The wind stung his face as he walked away from the wound in the earth, each step heavier than the last.

Months passed. Or maybe years. Elias could no longer tell. The city he returned to was unchanged—its towers rising defiantly against the sky, its lights glittering like distant stars. People bustled in the streets, their faces illuminated by neon and shadow, their laughter sharp and hollow in his ears. He wandered among them like a ghost, feeling disconnected, untethered from the world around him.

The memories clung to him like a second skin, creeping into his dreams and slipping into the silences between breaths. In the dead of night, he would wake drenched in sweat, his pulse racing, the scent of decay still sharp in his nostrils. He had stood on the edge of something vast and incomprehensible. And though he had returned, some part of him remained behind, lost forever in the endless dark.

Isabelle had tried to reach him at first. Her voice had been soft, patient, but eventually, it turned brittle. He couldn't tell her what he had seen, couldn't force the horrors into words without sounding mad. Eventually, she stopped asking, and the silence between them grew too heavy to bear. One day, she was simply gone, leaving behind a hollow space in their shared apartment and a faint scent of lavender on her pillow.

Elias turned to old books, ancient texts, anything that might give him clarity. He found scraps of lore, half-truths buried in myth, hints of civilizations that had teetered on the edge of the same abyss he had stared into. The names he found—the Architects, the Old Ones, the Harbingers—were fragments of something larger, a puzzle whose edges had been worn smooth by time.

But answers eluded him. Each discovery only led to more questions, each whispered revelation more chilling than the last. The entities he had faced were not the masters—they were merely servants, echoes of something older and infinitely worse. The gateway had been but a fragment, a crack in a much larger dam holding back an ocean of darkness.

The artifact sat on his desk, lifeless and cold, yet he couldn't bring himself to hide it away. It felt wrong to turn his back on it, as though it might wake while he slept, pulsing with that sickly green glow once more. Some nights, he swore he could hear it—a faint hum, almost imperceptible, vibrating against the edge of his hearing.

One evening, as rain hammered against the window, Elias found himself staring at his reflection in the glass. His eyes looked sunken, his hair unruly, streaked with grey that hadn't been there before. The city lights blurred into streaks of color across the pane, but in the distorted reflection, he saw something else—something vast and looming behind him, just out of focus.

He turned abruptly, but there was nothing there. Only the cold emptiness of his apartment.

The war wasn't over. The thought struck him suddenly, with the clarity of a knife slicing through fog. They had paused it, delayed it, but it wasn't finished. Somewhere, in the ruins of the Forbidden Worlds, the entities were stirring again. Their whispers crawled into his mind at night, faint but undeniable, like the ticking of some infernal clock counting down to the end of all things.

He didn't know when it would happen, or where. But it would.

Elias stepped away from the window and picked up the artifact from his desk. Its surface was cold, lifeless. But it felt heavy in his hand—too heavy for something so small.

The faces of those who had fought beside him flickered in his mind. Lyra's hollow eyes, Orin's steady hands, Damaris's fierce resolve. They had believed in something, fought for something, even as the shadows closed in around them.

He would keep fighting. He owed them that much.

As the rain continued to fall outside, Elias Thorne closed his hand around the

artifact and whispered a promise to the
darkness.

It wasn't over. And he would be ready.

334

Thank You

Dear Reader,

From the depths of my heart, thank you for embarking on this journey through Forbidden Worlds. Your time, imagination, and open mind mean more than words can truly express. Every page was written with the hope of sparking a sense of wonder, and it is readers like you who give these stories their true life.

I sincerely hope that this adventure has left you inspired, and that our paths will cross again in future books. Until then, may your own worlds—both real and imagined—always be full of mystery, magic, and discovery.

With heartfelt gratitude,

Edward Freeman